Roommate Wars

USA TODAY BESTSELLING AUTHOR

JULES BARNARD

JULESBARNARD.COM

Chapter One

Elise

I STEPPED INTO THE KITCHEN WITH MY SHOULDERS back and my head held high like I owned the place. Technically, I rented, but I had to show this apartment and its *inhabitants* who was in charge.

The kitchen's yellowing wallpaper cast a sallow glow, with one pitiful window that looked onto the concrete jungle of San Francisco's lower Pacific Heights. The neighborhood wasn't bad, with charming restaurants and architecture here and there, but not this building. This building sucked. But the apartment had been the only thing I could afford when I signed the lease two weeks ago. Now I understood why it was so damn cheap.

There was more than ugly wallpaper and grease-caked appliances to greet me in my new home.

I stormed across the kitchen and flung open the sink cabinet like Rambo preparing for battle. The roach motel sat exactly where I'd placed it last night to seduce my unwanted guests to their demise.

1

And those menaces were having none of it.

Roughly five black bodies the size of my thumb scurried from the light, avoiding the roach motel as if it were a contamination zone.

My skin crawled and my heart thumped. "Gah!" I flung the cabinet door shut and ran out of the room, hopping as though the ground were lava.

How did they know to avoid the trap?

Bang, bang, bang, came pounding on my living room wall, followed by a shout to *keep it down* mixed with an f-bomb.

Some of my new neighbors were nice, working-class folks. Others were scarier than my roaches. The guy next door fell in the second category. I'd only seen him from a distance. He was stocky, with unwashed hair, and wore the same dark-stained hooded sweatshirt and jeans every day, but it was his demeanor that had me hiding in my apartment. He turned his TV to max volume and played it throughout the night, but if I made so much as a peep, he complained through the thin walls.

As I contemplated my roach dilemma and tried to ignore my neighbor, another knock sounded, this one coming from the front door.

Normally my neighbor kept to yelling through walls, and that suited me because I did not want to encounter him face to face. Was he stepping up his game? My head grew woozy, and my hands began to sweat.

I was determined to live alone for the first time in my life, without student loans and without my sister's help, but it wasn't easy. Rent in San Francisco was astronomical, and my neighbors were unpredictable. Not to mention, the place I'd found had...issues.

More knocking sounded at the front door, and I

rubbed my eyes. I was exhausted after putting in a long day at my new job with the city health department, and no, it hadn't escaped my notice that I worked in public health and lived in a place that should probably be condemned.

I grabbed my phone and positioned my finger over the 911 emergency button, just in case, before I slowly opened the door with the chain latched.

Only the person on the other side wasn't my scary neighbor, or any of my neighbors.

"Jack?"

My sister's old roommate stood with one hand tucked into the front pocket of his jeans, a blue crewneck sweater stretching over an athletic build I'd secretly ogled when I visited my sister at her old place. The outfit was an upgrade from the sweatpants and holey T-shirts I usually saw him in. But his slightly ruffled, goldish-brown hair and piercing forest-green eyes were all Jack, set against an expression of inconvenience.

I hadn't seen Jack in months, as I was avoiding the man. He was literally the last person I wanted to find me here.

I glanced at the living room behind me. Everything I owned was a hand-me-down and on full display: a pleather recliner that had been hidden for a decade beneath Mom's clothes and other items back home and a wobbly white side table I'd pulled in off the street. No pictures. No plants. Nothing to make the place homey because I hadn't gotten around to that part. I also couldn't afford such luxuries. I would do anything to be independent, even suffer roaches, sketchy neighbors, and hand-me-down furniture. Didn't mean I wasn't embarrassed as hell that I couldn't afford better.

"You planning on letting me in?" He looked me in the

eye without a single fidget. I was the only one lacking confidence here.

Somehow Jack had discovered where I lived, and it wasn't like I was hiding anything; he was several inches taller and could look over my head. I unlatched the chain and opened the door wider.

He stepped inside, and his gaze scanned the living room, then landed on me like a stone. "This is where you chose to move? Your sister is worried, and I can see why."

From what my sister Sophia had said, Jack was wealthy, but you'd never know it from his living arrangement in a two-bedroom unit inside his best friend's building. It made sense he'd assume my shithole apartment was a choice. "Was there a point to your visit?" Given the roaches, my neighbor, and now Jack, my irritability was in peak form.

I hadn't expected my overprotective sister to send Jack to hunt me down. Sophia knew how tense things had been ever since the night I'd stayed over six months ago and sleepwalked into Jack's bedroom. I might have also accidentally-on-purpose landed on his penis. *Oops.* That one-night stand resulted in the worst walk of shame, and I was still recovering from both. Sophia must have been desperate to find me if she'd sent him along.

I intentionally hadn't given Sophia my new address until I could find time to spruce up the place. I couldn't get away with holding out forever, but I thought I'd make it past the first week.

Jack folded his arms loftily. He could pass for a normal tall guy—until he crossed his arms and the biceps popped out. Underneath those casual clothes were well-defined muscles and a swimmer's build I was trying to forget. "Sophia's worried."

"Nothing to worry about," I said with fake cheer. Ever

since that night, I'd been extremely awkward around Jack, and now was no different. Especially when memories of his naked body flashed before my eyes. My brow wrinkled as I considered something else. "How'd you find me here, anyway?"

His expression turned bland. "I asked around."

I eyed him suspiciously. "I made it a point to not tell anyone my new address, so what do you mean you *asked around*?"

He stepped farther into the small space, ignoring my question. "What's that smell?"

"Curry. From my neighbor across the hall."

"No, that smells good. I'm talking about the odor." He peeked inside the kitchen, his nose curling.

Oh, *that smell*. Yeah, that smell had been around since the day I moved in, and I didn't want to think too hard about its origin.

"No idea what you're talking about, and I take offense to your suggesting my place stinks." I tucked the wool scarf primly around my neck. September in San Francisco could be blazing or it could be nippy. These things became apparent when your heater was on the fritz.

Jack let out a low sigh, taking in my bundled-up appearance. "It's freezing in here, Elise. Why isn't your furnace on?"

"I turned it down to save money." He didn't need to know just how decrepit my place was. He'd run back to the flat he rented from his best friend—my sister's *boyfriend*—and blab. Sophia would then find out and insist I move in with her and Max in his lush apartment on the top floor of his Victorian building, and that wasn't happening. I needed personal independence. "I have lots of sweatshirts and thick socks, so no worries."

He studied me so long a chill ran down my arms, reminding me of other chills he'd elicited via sexy, tender touches a few months ago. Damn those memories!

I forced my gaze blank. "Feel free to tell Sophia I'm safe and sound and will be in touch soon. Anything else I can do for you?"

His eyes narrowed and held for a beat. "Why are you so stubborn?"

Jack Townsend had been relaxed around my sister, but for some reason, I agitated him. Well, the feeling was mutual. We must bring out the worst in each other. Except the night he'd worshiped my body like a temple...

I needed to stop thinking of that night.

"Why are you so bossy?" I tilted my head and blinked several times, glaring in a way I hoped spelled doom for him.

He sighed as though he was tired of my antics. "I've never been bossy. Not even with my employees."

Jack's business comings and goings were somewhat of a mystery. I'd only recently learned he owned an entire company. No idea what the guy did, since I'd only seen him when I visited Sophia, and back then, he'd been milling around the kitchen searching for food in his bare feet or playing video games with Max.

A devious look crossed his face. "I need to use your bathroom." He strode across the living room, then stopped abruptly and retraced his steps over the squishy floorboard I made a practice of walking around for fear of dropping onto my downstairs neighbor's lap.

Jack bounced on the floorboard, and it gave way too much. I rubbed my forehead, and he cut me a look. "Nice flooring you got here."

Yes, the floor was a problem. But not the biggest.

Jack continued down the hallway.

"Wait!" I ran after him. "The flush is a little tricky. It takes a tender touch. I'll get it after you're finished."

He stepped inside the tiny bathroom, which required tucking one's arms in to turn, and closed the door in my face.

Shit. He'd picked up on the smell, the floorboard, and now he'd know there was an issue with the toilet. Also, exactly what personal crap had I forgotten to put away in there?

I performed mental gymnastics, running through the space: toothpaste on the sink, panda shower cap on the door hook, hair bands in a jewelry bowl—nothing too egregious. Except—

I slapped my hand over my mouth, biting back a scream. I'd left out the bleach for the peach fuzz above my lip on the counter!

Son. Of. A. Bitch.

I'd never lived with a guy. In fact, no man had ever come over to my place because I'd always lived with my hoarder mom in the Sunset District, and now that I thought about it, some of the stuff in my bathroom was mortifying.

Jack was still hot, but my crush had ended the night we slept together. I'd purged him from my system through meaningless sex. Fine, I was in the *process* of purging, but even so, this was just awkward. Crush or no crush, no woman wanted a man to know her hygiene habits.

"You almost done in there?" I paced the hallway. And then I heard it. The sound of the toilet tank cover scraping over the base. *Noooo!* "Jack! What are you doing?"

He let out what sounded like a frustrated groan, then said, "What the hell, Elise?" He opened the bathroom door so fast I nearly fell onto his broad chest. "What is going on here?" His green eyes were darker than normal, and his full, kissable lips were set like granite.

My mouth formed a silent O. "What? Not everyone has a place as nice as yours."

"Your apartment is a piece of shit. I wouldn't let my dog live here."

"You don't own a dog."

"And what's the deal with the furnace? You didn't just turn it down; you turned it off. It smells damp. Actually—" He looked over my shoulder into the small one-bedroom we San Franciscans called a "junior one-bedroom," because it was essentially a closet we stuffed a bed in. His nose wrinkled. "Is that black mold?"

Shit, shit. I stepped backward and reached behind me, fumbling with the bedroom doorknob and trying to close the door. "It's mildew. No biggie."

He pushed past me and opened the door, where more of my single-lady paraphernalia lay haphazardly: undies drying on a drying rack, though they wouldn't dry because it *was* too damp and cold in here, plus mounds of blankets to prove him right about the furnace.

He grabbed my hand and dragged me down the short hallway. "You can't stay here. It's toxic."

I karate-chopped his hand, and he pulled back with a wince. "Don't tell me what to do, Jack Townsend."

He rolled his eyes. "Elise, people get sick from black mold. I'm surprised you haven't noticed symptoms. It's toxic to even be standing here."

"Symptoms?" I said, as though I didn't know what he was talking about. I was a registered nurse with a master's in public health. I knew. I'd just been ignoring the chronic headache, brain fog, and weird metallic taste until a better apartment came along—which I was desperately working to find. No point in telling him he was right and that I'd slept with a mask at night since the day I moved in. Or that I'd been begging my new landlord to fix the furnace.

The place had been fine when I checked it out a month ago, but apparently things could go south fast. It didn't help that my apartment had been occupied when I viewed it, with the mold situation hidden behind furniture and drapes.

"Like a chronic headache, that sort of thing?" he prodded.

Was he some sort of mind reader? He was supposed to be the easygoing guy my sister roomed with for a few months. When the hell had he become intuitive? Or knowledgeable about toxic mold?

I waved my hand. "I'll buy bleach and take care of it."

"You'd need more than bleach; you'd need a hazmat suit." As though he'd just reminded himself of how bad it was, he looped his arm around my back and shuffled me to the front door.

"Hey!" I said and took a step back.

"We're leaving, Elise." His expression was pure masculine obstinance.

I planted my feet. "You're leaving. This is where I live."

He shot me a look that had my hackles rising. Because that look was calculating. "I have an extra bedroom now that your sister moved in with Max. You can stay at my place while your landlord takes care of this"—he looked around in disgust—"situation."

Hell to the *no*. Had he lost his mind?

Jack's apartment was only a floor below where my sister lived with Max. Not to mention the *living with Jack* part. I was trying to get over my crush, but I hadn't quite succeeded. He was beautiful, and he'd been incredible in bed. These were temptations only the strongest of independent women could overlook, and I was determined to be one of them. "I'll pass."

His mouth twisted in annoyance. "Still thinking about that night, are you? It wasn't that good. I've entirely forgotten about it."

My face heated and a twinge of pain shot through my stomach. *It wasn't that good?*

A memory flashed of Jack gently gripping my face and passionately kissing me, his tongue teasing my mouth while his hands roamed. I'd quivered at that kiss, and the sex had been explosive...and he'd just said *he didn't remember it?*

Asshole!

"It'll only be for a month," he continued and checked the time on his phone, as though what we were discussing wasn't the major upheaval I didn't need. "Just long enough for you to find a decent alternative."

A woman had her pride. "No."

Bad sex? Was he trying to piss me off?

He lifted his eyebrow. "Not even rent-free?"

Say what?

Chapter Two

Elise

"One month, no rent," he said, his mouth twisting slightly as though he knew he'd snagged me with that last bit.

Money was the one thing I didn't joke about. "Are you pitying me? Offering me a room because my apartment sucks?"

His life depended on the answer, because pity was the one thing I couldn't handle. Not from anyone. I was competent, dammit.

A mixture of fear and disbelief crossed his face. "Have you met your sister? If she finds out I walked away and left you here, she will kill me. Then Max will stomp on me with his Ferragamo oxfords for upsetting his girlfriend. This is sheer survival on my part. Besides, it's only temporary." He looked around with a snarl. "If you lasted a week here, surely you can survive a month with me."

How had he known I'd been here a week? Was he stalking me?

And I wasn't so sure I could survive a month with him. That was a very long time when lingering attraction was involved.

"I won't be around much," he continued. "I hired a new CEO to free up time for other projects. I'll be working long hours, getting her up to speed. You'll practically have the place to yourself."

Free up his time? Last I saw, the man practically lived at home, roaming around in sweatpants. And why was I actually considering this? "Look, it's nice of you to offer, but I don't like owing people."

His gaze narrowed as though he were calculating. "Not even if the free rent was in exchange for taking care of a few things around the house? I don't want to hire someone I don't trust."

"And you trust me?" My voice cracked on that last part.

He blinked as though I'd caught him in a lie. "I trust you with the place," he finally said.

Which was as good as admitting he didn't trust me in other ways.

I deserved that. This man had rocked me off-balance, and I'd run after our night together. Not exactly a winning response. But if the sex had been so forgettable for him, then my lingering feelings were a moot point. It still stung to hear he didn't care.

This was a truly terrible idea, but I couldn't ignore the financial benefit. If Jack was gone most of the time, it wouldn't be so bad, would it?

He shifted his feet as though growing impatient. "In addition to helping me out, you'll be giving your sister peace of mind. I won't tell her where I found you."

Okay, now he was bringing out the big guns. Not telling my sister about this place was a massive concession because it rivaled our mother's hoarder house before we'd fixed it up. "One month?"

"In exchange for help around the house."

Oh, I didn't like the sound of that. It was too vague. There was definitely a catch.

We slept together the one night I'd sleepwalked into his bedroom, and it had been a low point for me. Not because of the sex, but because I'd practically thrown myself at him after crushing on the man for weeks when visiting my sister. A small part of me worried he'd complied that night to be nice. Or because, you know, easy booty call. He sure as hell had never acted as though he liked me before then.

Though he'd surrendered enthusiastically to my advances, so at least there was that.

In any case, given our history, "help around the house" could mean more than taking out the trash. "What exactly are you expecting? I'm not going to warm your bed, Jack." He'd called the sex forgettable, but men made funny decisions when easy access was involved.

He drew back, offended. "What sort of man do you take me for?"

"A red-blooded one."

The corners of his mouth pulled back, and he glanced down. "Fair. But no, that's not what I had in mind. I was thinking more along the lines of you taking care of the laundry and dishes. Maybe cooking dinner five nights a week." He glanced around nervously. "Can we negotiate in the hallway? I feel mold spores making a bed in my lungs."

I crossed my arms. "No."

His sigh came out on a low growl. "I have a cleaning person who comes twice a month," he said. "They give the place a deep clean, including your bedroom and bathroom."

Free rent for a month, no black mold, plus someone to

clean my bathroom? I wasn't sure I trusted Jack, but he was speaking my language. "What else do you want from me?"

He shrugged. "Nothing. Your sister would want me to help if I could. She already said you refused to move in with her."

And living with Jack would be downstairs from her, where she could burrow all up in my business. "This is a terrible idea."

"Do you have a better one?" His look was pure challenge.

I didn't, and he knew it.

"It's only a month," he said again. "It'll fly by before you know it." Something must have caught his eye because he flinched.

I glanced at where he was looking. "Oh, that's just Jack, my roach."

His jaw shifted. "You named a cockroach after me?"

"You have a problem with that?"

Two more roaches scurried across the permanently sticky hardwood. "Fuck!" he said, moving farther away. "Maybe the rest of the people in this building should move out too."

I glanced at my nails, unbothered. "I checked. My apartment is the worst. The others don't have—" I waved in the direction of the black-mold wall. "There's a leak somewhere in this unit, so it's just special."

He ran stiff fingers through his hair. "Are you coming or not?"

It was clearly making him nervous standing in my apartment. I must have a high tolerance for filth and critters after living with Mom for so long. Still, I hesitated. This wouldn't be living with my sister or mom, but I'd still be mooching off another human being.

He sighed. "If this is about that night, can't you just forget about it?"

My eyes widened. "Can you?"

He looked off, not meeting my gaze. "Course I can. I'm a man."

I wasn't sure I believed him, but if that were true, it bothered me. Even if forgetting was what I wanted, that night was burned into my brain, and I didn't like that he could so casually forget.

"It's already forgotten," I said, and prayed the lie didn't show on my face.

"Good." He looked down my body. "Because you're not my type. Don't worry about anything happening."

Again, *ouch*. Yet, somehow, his words reassured me. He didn't want to go there, and I didn't either. I wasn't in the right mindset for a relationship, and something told me being in one with Jack would be a maelstrom. This was a business transaction, nothing more.

No matter what I'd told myself over the last week to stay put and not go running back to Mom's, I *was* desperate to find something safer. If Jack's place was a temporary stopover, would that be so bad?

He looked around. "Leave your stuff. It's probably got mold spores. We'll figure out what to do with it later. For now, we'll get you new clothes, or you can borrow from your sister."

"I'm not taking a single thing from my sister." Sophia had worked her ass off, and this year was her time to focus on herself.

His mouth flattened. "Then you can wear one of my T-shirts. Happy?"

Not at all. His shirts smelled like him, and if memory served, he smelled amazing.

Everything about Jack was what had me scurrying down the fire escape the morning after we'd slept together. I'd felt protected and cherished in his arms—something I'd never experienced before. And that had been terrifying.

Jack scratched the back of his neck like he had the creepy-crawlies. "So what's it going to be? Are you coming?"

"I don't cook. You'll have to deal with whatever I make. And it's three nights a week, not five." I hated cooking.

He nodded. "That works."

This was a stupid idea I'd probably regret. "Fine. I'm coming."

Chapter Three

Jack

ELISE SHUT THE DOOR TO HER APARTMENT, A LARGE purse slung from her shoulder—the only item I'd allowed her to bring. And even that I planned to fumigate before it entered my place.

She eyed me as she walked down the cracked concrete stairs, using the rusty iron railing for support. "You look like a cat that got the cream. You better not be up to something, Jack."

I had ulterior motives, but not the ones she assumed. I couldn't stand her living in that apartment. It was a disaster zone. She'd been bundled up like she was living in the Midwest in winter, not San Francisco in the fall. The infestation of roaches and mold had been the tipping point.

Fuck, she was stubborn. I'd had to come up with all kinds of crap on the fly to get her to cooperate. Including moving her in with me, which had been the only quick solution. And even that hadn't been easy.

I'd told her I didn't find her attractive, then nearly

gave the lie away by checking her out. Elise was beautiful, with dark hair and liquid brown eyes that spewed fire when I pissed her off, which was often. She was fiercely independent, and her ornery nature was something that both amused and annoyed me. She was a pain in the ass to get to cooperate, and I wasn't about to give her another reason to not move in. I would have said anything to get her out of that toxic place, including denying I felt anything for her after our night together.

I reached for her bag, and she glared at my hand. "I appreciate your independence," I said. "Now, will you please let me carry this for you?"

The corners of her mouth pulled back wryly. "Since you asked so nicely."

Holding her purse between my thumb and forefinger, I walked her to the car and opened the passenger-side door. "There's nothing nefarious going on, Elise. You have trust issues."

She delivered another narrow-eyed look. "The only reason I'm agreeing to this is because I get more out of it than you do."

We'll see about that.

She leaned forward as though she'd heard my silent thought.

I kept my expression bland and gestured for her to step inside my slightly dinged Audi Q4 that was small enough to park on most San Francisco streets.

A second later, she sank into the passenger seat, and I shut the door, gusting out a breath of air.

Thank fuck. I thought I'd never get her out of there.

I walked around the back of the car, popped the trunk, and wrapped her purse inside a blanket. I'd contact one of

Max's friends who worked in mold remediation later and ask him what to do with it.

———

THE TRIP across town was quiet except for Elise's heavy sighs that made me worry she was a hairsbreadth from reneging on our agreement. I really didn't want her going back to her apartment, so I climbed up the stairs of the Victorian ahead of her to keep her moving forward.

I opened the door to the place I'd rented from Max for the last few years, and Elise hesitated.

I took in the space with fresh eyes: kitchen on the left, across from a small dining area I never used, and the living room Max had spent a fortune remodeling after one of my renters trashed the place.

A year and a half ago, I'd made a poor choice in both my roommate and the woman I dated. Mainly because they were one and the same. A pretty, seemingly desperate woman had come looking for a room and needed something affordable. Cue my rescue instincts.

And here I was doing it again.

Only Elise wasn't like women I've dated in the past, and certainly not like a typical roommate. For one, she almost never did what I asked and refused to take me up on anything I offered.

The women I'd dated had been on the selfish side and accepted every gift that came their way. There was something reassuring about relationships with people I'd never be in love with. No need to worry about getting too close. But those shallow connections were bound to bite me in the ass, and eventually one did.

It hadn't taken me long to realize my mistake in dating

a roommate. I broke things off, but not before she went out with a bang. While I was away on a business trip, she hosted a rager that got out of hand and nearly burned down the building. Hence Max's need to remodel, since his unit was directly above mine and had been damaged too.

Max was low-key about money, but I'd never forgive myself for allowing someone like that to live with me. If she'd only hurt me, I could deal. But because she'd hurt someone I cared about, that was a hard *no*.

Yet here I was, opening up the place to another needy woman.

Only this one was different. Elise wasn't shallow or self-ish. I'd practically had to drag her out of her dump of an apartment. It took all my energy to keep calm and work out an arrangement the stubborn woman would agree to, when all I wanted was to throw her over my shoulder and haul her ass out of there.

God, she was infuriating. I hadn't gone there with the intent of asking Elise to live with me. I'd gone there because Sophia couldn't find her sister, and I didn't like that. The situation was suspect, with no one knowing where Elise lived.

Fine, I'd also been worried.

And for good reason! I'd pulled a few strings and found out Elise had been living in that apartment for an entire week. A week in that shit-heap... It was enough to put me in a rage.

I squeezed my forehead and motioned Elise into the apartment. "Make yourself at home."

She walked past me and looked around. "It's exactly the same."

"You expected something else?"

Her face sank a touch. "No, it's nice. You have a comfortable place, Jack."

My chest tightened. There was danger in inviting Elise to live with me. She wasn't materialistic. She was down-to-earth and feisty. If I wanted a relationship, she was the type of woman I'd choose. But nothing had changed in that department. I *didn't* want a serious relationship. Not ever. Shallow relationships were all I could handle.

She picked at the pilled and faded sweatshirt she wore as though she were uncomfortable, then unwound the scarf from around her neck.

I reached for her scarf. "I'll take your clothes."

She raised an eyebrow. "Excuse me?"

That hadn't come out right. I cleared my throat. "I'll have them dry-cleaned."

Her disbelief grew. "You'll have my sweatshirt and moth-eaten wool scarf dry-cleaned?"

My mouth twisted. "Right. Laundered, then."

A touch of fire lit behind her eyes. "Are you calling me contaminated?"

"One hundred percent."

She frowned.

"We should wash everything after you lived in that apartment." Her frown deepened, and I squeezed the back of my neck. "I'll buy you new stuff, okay?"

She crossed her arms. "Not okay. I don't need you to buy me clothes."

Said no woman ever. "Then grab some of mine." My voice rose, and I reminded myself to calm the fuck down.

I took a deep breath. No one riled me up like Elise. She was beautiful and stubborn. Or maybe just proud. Either way... A. Pain. In. The. Ass.

"You know that place you found wasn't safe. Why are

you even arguing with me?"

She looked away. "Whatever. Can I use your shower?"

"You can use *your* shower."

Her face brightened. "That's right. I have my own now. I always liked Sophia's bathroom. Max put in all that pretty marble."

"He has good taste," I said absently. "Now, about the clothes..."

"Fine." She pulled off the scarf and dropped it on the hardwood floor. "I will *borrow* a few things until I get my clothes back."

She wasn't getting her clothes back because I was going to have them incinerated so no one would be exposed to the shit in her last apartment. But I wasn't about to tell her that. "We'll talk about it later. Go shower."

Her eyes narrowed at the command, but she turned and walked down the hallway toward the bedrooms. She paused in front of mine before heading inside her own.

Thinking about the night we set the sheets on fire? Or maybe that was wishful thinking on my part.

I'd lied my ass off and told her I didn't think about that night, but I thought about it. A lot. Was having a hard time *not* thinking about it.

I rubbed my forehead. What was I doing? Elise's moving in was a shitshow waiting to happen, but the alternative and her staying in her apartment had been unacceptable. I wasn't kidding about Sophia killing me if I hadn't gotten Elise out of there. Of course, that was only half the reason.

I would have done it no matter what because I cared about what happened to Elise.

I stormed out, needing air. Space. How was I going to live with this woman?

Chapter Four

Jack

I WAS STANDING ON THE LANDING OUTSIDE MY apartment, attempting to clear my head, when Max sauntered down the stairs in a three-piece charcoal suit. My best friend dressed to impress every day, but he reserved the three-pieces for special clients. "Big meeting?"

He straightened his tie absently. His dark hair was combed back—a stark contrast to his light eyes. "I'm wooing a group for a project south of Market." He paused. "What's going on? You look stressed."

I was normally the even-keeled type. "Elise moved in." I tilted my head toward the apartment. "She's taking over Sophia's old room."

Max's eyes widened. "Is that a good idea?"

"Nope."

"I see... Is she okay?"

"Presumably."

Max nodded. "When are you going to tell Sophia?"

"I'd hoped Elise would."

Max checked his watch. "I'm late for the meeting. Make sure you let Sophia know, or I'll tell her. Either way, she should know." He lifted his chin. "Catch me up later on how this all came about."

I waved without looking and leaned my forearms against the banister. My head was about to explode. I'd been standing out here for nearly an hour and was no clearer on what I was doing.

I waited until Max disappeared down the stairs, then took a deep breath and headed back into the apartment. Elise should be showered and settled by now.

Only, she was nowhere in sight. I closed the door, and my chest loosened. Considering how Elise had handled the aftermath of our one-night stand, she was going to avoid me as much as I avoided her.

Maybe this wouldn't be so bad. We could keep our distance if I planned things right.

I headed into the kitchen, hankering for something salty. Sophia had kept the salty garbage stocked when she lived here. I suspected she did that for my benefit, as I hadn't wanted to venture out back then. I'd been dealing with the aftermath of my ex nearly destroying the building and my ass-poor taste in women, and for a less obvious reason that I hadn't shared with anyone yet.

With Sophia living with Max, I was forced to buy my own crap food these days, and I'd been remiss in keeping up supplies. Hence the absence of salt and my current dilemma.

I pulled out my phone and ordered groceries from a delivery app. I couldn't miss my meeting this afternoon, but now that Elise was living here, I should make sure there was food. At least for this first week.

Until she got settled.

And had a chance to shop.

Then she was on her own.

"Shit." It was going to be hard to not want to take care of Elise. I didn't know why I felt protective of her, but I did.

"Why 'shit'?" came her voice as she swept around the corner carrying the clothes she'd worn to my apartment. And wearing my boxers and T-shirt.

My mouth went dry and my eyes nearly bugged out of my head—which I promptly cleared, because controlling myself was essential to this scheme.

The boxers were loose on her waist and slightly fitting over curvy hips. She'd tied one of my holey T-shirts into a knot at the front so it didn't drape to her thighs. Her hair was still wet, loose strands dripping water onto the thin T-shirt and leaving almost transparent patches over her chest, making it clear she'd ditched the bra.

I slammed my eyes closed. This living arrangement was going to be hell.

Elise dropped her things near the front door. When she turned and headed for the couch, I stealthily kicked the clothes outside.

I feigned searching the fridge. "I see you found something to wear."

"Yep. Thanks, by the way." There was a pause, then, "What kind of laundry detergent do you use?"

That caught me off guard. I looked over. "Huh?"

She was sniffing my T-shirt, her expression unadulterated pleasure.

And she might as well have licked my cock.

"You always smell so good, but I can't place the detergent. I better get familiar with it if I'm to do the laundry."

I don't know why her liking the way I smelled got my

blood pumping, but it did. "I have no idea," I said, acting like I didn't care.

She shrugged. "I guess I'll use whatever." She plopped on the couch Max had shelled out ten grand for because he "needed something comfortable" on his daily visits, and kicked her bare feet up onto the coffee table, crossing her lightly tanned, sexy-as-hell legs. She'd done this a million times when her sister lived here. But never while wearing my boxers that barely hit mid-thigh.

Fuuuuck...

Someone rang the doorbell, and I wiped the bead of sweat that had formed on my forehead. *Thank the grocery gods.* That was quick even for the neighborhood food delivery, who were pretty damn prompt.

"I'll get it," I said, but Elise was already surfing the TV, not paying attention.

I opened the door, but it wasn't the grocery person. "Thalia?"

My new CEO smiled in a way that made the corners of her eyes crinkle, and I suspected it was her secret sauce for making power deals and coming across genuine. She had shoulder-length, no-nonsense, light-brown hair, and cut a fine figure in the professional world. She was young but not too young, and not so good-looking that people (men) didn't take her seriously. Sadly, those things mattered at her career level. Though I would have hired her regardless.

I checked the time on my phone. I wasn't running late, despite my impromptu new housemate. "I thought we were meeting at the office."

"Oh, we were, we were," Thalia said and swatted the air congenially. "But I was in the neighborhood." She glanced behind her, smiling as though she found the street charming. "I know you prefer working from home, so I thought I'd pop on by."

Elise's neck was stretched like a meerkat as she watched us. I couldn't tell if she was curious or if there was more behind her scrutiny.

I stepped back and let Thalia in. This wasn't the best time, but I'd be spending weeks getting her up to speed. Might as well introduce her to Elise, because my new CEO was correct: I vastly preferred working from my home office. "Thalia, this is Elise, my new roommate. Elise, this is Thalia, the CEO of my VR company, Environ."

Elise greeted Thalia, then flashed me a questioning look. "VR?"

"A virtual reality company that predicts the impacts of natural disasters."

Elise's forehead scrunched. "Is this the company you own with Max?"

I shifted and tucked a hand in my pocket. "No—that's another company." I glanced between the two women uncomfortably. I liked to have my hands in multiple pots to keep from getting bored, but it was unusual. "There are a few."

Thalia nodded and winked.

Given how thoroughly she'd reviewed Environ, I wouldn't be surprised if my new CEO knew everything about my other businesses. The woman was a shark.

Elise stood. "Can I get you anything to drink?" she asked Thalia.

I winced. Should have offered first. "Do you need anything?" I said belatedly.

Thalia shook her head. "No, I'm fine and ready to get started."

"Okay, well..." I rubbed my jaw. "I guess we can head

back to my office." I really hadn't thought this through, considering my office was in my bedroom, but it would have to do.

"Certainly," Thalia said brightly.

I felt Elise's gaze as I walked to my bedroom.

My apartment wasn't the idyllic location for professional meetings, and I wished Thalia had given me a heads-up. I would have instructed her to keep the meeting at the office. But I did have numbers on our newest prospective client handy. And my bedroom was a large master suite, with a separate nook that fit my office furniture and a small couch. It wasn't entirely unprofessional.

And then I remembered Elise had been the last woman in my bedroom...

This was a business meeting. Why was I feeling guilty? It wasn't like Elise and I were dating. No way would I get involved with another roommate, and especially not her.

Thalia entered the room and passed the bed I'd remembered to make this morning. She headed straight for the nook that housed my large desk and three massive computer monitors. The desk stood in front of a window overlooking the street, with a distant view of the bay.

"I can see why you enjoy working here," Thalia said. "Nice view." She pulled out a folder and sank onto the couch that faced the window and not my bedroom.

This wasn't so bad. I could make it work.

Besides, I'd needed the distraction from Elise and her legs, so in a sense, Thalia's timing was perfect.

Chapter Five

Elise

I was scavenging in Jack's kitchen for food when the universe heard my prayer and sent a delivery woman bearing groceries.

I graciously accepted said food on his behalf, decided this was too much for him to eat alone, and helped myself to a sandwich after I put everything away.

It was somewhat strange that Jack had invited his CEO into his bedroom, but then again, this was Jack we were talking about. A dedicated homebody.

I'd gotten a glimpse of his bedroom the one night I spent there, and then earlier when I borrowed some clothes. His room was massive, and half of it was set up like an office, so it wasn't entirely unusual that he'd have a meeting there.

Who was I kidding? It *was* strange. But I batted down any territorial instincts I was feeling toward Jack because he wasn't mine, even if I felt a twinge of something unpleasant in my chest at watching another woman go to his room.

This was strictly a one-month business transaction

where I made dinner three nights out of the week and did laundry. No bedroom shenanigans involved. That bridge had been burned.

Twenty minutes later, the sound of the woman's laughter made my ears perk up. Because her tone was flirty.

What in the hell were they doing in there?

I tiptoed to my bedroom and closed the door, leaving it open a crack, then sank onto the bed my sister had left behind and listened.

Was I being nosey? Damn straight!

Jack was hot—when he wasn't bossing me around. I'd seen the way Thalia looked at him, and it hadn't been entirely professional.

She was classy-looking, dressed in moss-green wide-leg slacks and a matching blazer with a sexy cream tank. Her outfit was the kind of top-notch businesswoman gear I'd never worn in my life, because who could afford that shit? Jack's new CEO, apparently.

Meanwhile, I was in boxers and a ratty T-shirt, so I didn't feel uncomfortable. No, not at all.

This was my temporary home. Everyone dressed like crap at home. I didn't need to look good; I needed a roof over my head, and who cared if his CEO was classy and pretty? All I wanted was my independence, and living with Jack was a means to an end. If this lady had designs on him, it was good I knew that from the start, so I didn't get in the way.

I sighed and looked around. Other than the bed, my room was barren, and I couldn't find my phone. Or my purse, come to think of it. I'd dumped the clothes I'd been wearing near the front door after my shower, and Jack had stashed them somewhere when I wasn't looking.

As much as I hated to admit it, he'd been right about not

bringing anything from the moldy apartment. But I needed something to wear to work tomorrow. Maybe I could pick up a few basics from Target?

I tiptoed into the living room and looked around for my purse. Jack had done something with it after we left my apartment, and I forgot to ask him for it when we got here, as the idea of living with him was throwing me off.

I looked to the ceiling and sighed. I couldn't buy basic clothing for tomorrow if I didn't have a wallet. Should I interrupt them and ask him what he'd done with it?

I returned to the hallway and stared at Jack's door. The sound of his deep voice filtered out as he said something about synergistic outreach—whatever that meant. I'd be disturbing their meeting to ask about my purse, which was a weird roommate thing to do.

Fine, I thought and yawned. This could wait until later.

I crumpled like an accordion on Sophia's old mattress and closed my eyes.

When I stirred briefly sometime later, it was to the feel of a soft, fluffy blanket being draped over me, right before I sank into a dreamless sleep.

———

"Morning," I said as I entered the kitchen the next day. "Thank you for the blanket." I'd left my door open a crack last night, and Jack must have given me one at some point.

He was sitting at the counter scarfing cereal and scrolling through his phone. "No worries," he said without looking up.

I opened the pantry. "Do you know what happened to my purse? I couldn't find it last night."

After I nodded off yesterday afternoon, I'd slept straight

through the night. Living in the roach and mold apartment was stressful, but damn, that was a lot of sleep.

He crunched on a mouthful of some kind of granola/cornflake combo and said, "It's gone."

I blinked several times, and my heart began to pound. "Gone? My purse has my work access card and phone, along with my credit cards. It can't be gone."

For a second he stopped chewing, his gaze darting to the side. Then he proceeded to shove another bite in his mouth. "It's getting fumigated by a guy who knows a guy that Max put me in touch with."

My eyes widened. "What? Jackson, you can't just take my stuff."

"Name's not Jackson, just Jack." He glanced up, finally looking at me. "Don't they know you at the health department? Will they need to see the badge to let you in?"

There was probably someone I could call, though it wouldn't look good to have lost my badge right after starting the job. "That's beside the point. You can't take my things and do what you want with them. Those were my personal belongings! My purse has my driver's license and phone and money."

He gulped orange juice, his muscular throat working the liquid down, and I glanced away. There was a reason I'd had a crush on Sophia's old roommate—and it was because he was hot as hell. Even his throat, damn him. I was furious, but my hormones had a mind of their own.

He set the glass on the marble countertop. "Driver's license? You don't own a car; you take the bus to work."

How the hell did he know that?

I threw up my hands. "I need my money. And I have no clothes!" I was still wearing the boxers and T-shirt he'd lent me yesterday.

He finally took me in, and his gaze snagged on my legs before he lifted the bowl to his mouth and drank the cereal milk like a savage.

"Jackson, are you listening?"

He cut me a glare. "Are you going to keep calling me that?"

Finally, something I said got his attention. "Yes. It's catchy."

"You'll never get your purse back with that attitude."

I breathed in and counted to ten, then let out the air. I would kill him after I got my purse back, but not before. "I can't go to work looking like this. I have a professional job."

He stood and carried his dish to the sink, where he rinsed it under the water. "Borrow more of my stuff. I'm sure you can do something with one of my button-down shirts."

Okay, that could work. "What about pants?"

"Your sister is on her way down. Borrow a pair of hers."

"*What?*"

Right on cue, my sister stormed into the apartment, carrying her giant, all-purpose bag, her hair already frizzy even though it was only seven thirty in the morning. "Where have you been?" Her face was flushed, her expression concerned.

He'd called Sophia? Jack was dead.

And if he thought I'd stop calling him that ridiculous nickname, he had another thing coming. This was a trap. He'd brought me here to torture me with my sister's over-protectiveness, and it was about to backfire on his ass.

I smiled reassuringly at Soph. "I was a little busy. Sorry for not getting in touch sooner."

Sophia dumped her bag on the counter, and it landed

with a thud that sounded like she might have broken her laptop. "You couldn't return a phone call?"

"I was working and moving. You went through the same thing not that long ago. You know how hard it can be."

Her expression softened into one of disappointment. "But I could have helped. You didn't need to do it all on your own."

Which was why I hadn't called her. My sister had mothering issues.

I loved Sophia dearly, and she was my best friend, but sometimes her nurturing went too far. Especially when I wanted to stand on my own.

Though, I had to admit, I could use her help if I was to make it to work on time. "Well, now's your chance. Can I borrow a pair of pants?"

Chapter Six

Elise

I RETURNED HOME LATER THAT AFTERNOON TO FIND Jack hanging out with Max, each wearing virtual reality goggles. The two of them were walking around the living room like tourists admiring architecture.

This wasn't an unfamiliar scenario. I'd tried out VR goggles when Sophia lived here. At the time, I'd checked out a video game Jack designed, and it had been super fun. Though whatever game they were playing now seemed tamer than the last one, which had involved swords.

I closed the front door, and Jack must have had the volume set to low, because he lifted his headset and turned to me. "You're home?" He checked the time on his phone, and his eyes rounded. "Wow, I didn't realize it was this late."

Max pulled off his headset and set it on the coffee table. "I should get going," he said. But instead of leaving, he reached for a handful of cheese crackers from a bowl and jammed them in his mouth, taking his sweet time.

Jack's gaze dipped to my pants before he snickered and looked away. "I see Sophia hooked you up. She's shorter than you, right?"

My mouth compressed. Must he trigger me at every turn? Jack was the reason I had no clothes! "She's five foot five," I pointed out, defending my current fashion look.

"And you're, what? Five-eight."

It was smooth that he knew that right off the bat. "Yes."

"Which explains the flood situation you have going on."

I clenched my hands together and closed my eyes. "Do you know how embarrassing it was walking around like this?"

He shrugged. "The shirt looks good."

The shirt was his, the ass. And yes, it was pretty cute, rolled up at the sleeves and unbuttoned at the top with a camisole underneath. But the pants were another story. "These pants are skinners, showing every line of my underwear"—was that a blush from Jackson?—"and yes, there is a flood in the house, and not in a cute, fashionable way. The pants are pencil style. They look ridiculous stopping halfway up my calves."

He turned to Max, who'd been silently watching our exchange. "Thoughts?"

Max grabbed another handful of crackers and made his way to the door. "I make no comments about my girlfriend's wardrobe because she looks incredible in everything."

Jack and I exchanged a revolted look. Probably the only thing we agreed on was how nauseating Sophia and Max were together.

"I need my clothes back." I swung my head in Max's direction. "Any chance I can get a lift to my old apartment?"

"Hell no," Jack said and moved in front of me. "Let's go, Elise. We're getting you something to wear."

———

"WHAT DO YOU THINK OF THIS?" I asked Jack, holding up black slacks from the sale rack.

After a bit of bickering in the car, I'd convinced him I needed to go to Target and not a mall. He'd seemed confused, but he hadn't seen the balance in my savings account.

He looked at the pants and shrugged lightly. "They look okay." He glanced around, his brow furrowed. "Why do I feel like I've done this before?"

"Shopping at Target?" I asked as I checked the price tag.

"No." He waved his hand choppily. "I've done this before—bought women's clothes. Only with your sister when she lived in the apartment." He pouted adorably. "I am not a personal shopper."

"This was your idea. If you recall, I wanted to return to my apartment and the items I left behind." I lifted a blue blouse that had gaudy orange flowers on it. It wasn't my style, but I wanted to see his reaction.

His mouth twisted as though he'd eaten something bitter, and he turned his thumb down.

Okay, so his taste was on point. No wonder Soph had used him when she needed fashion advice.

"Think of it as a window into a woman's life," I said. "This will help you with your dating situation."

He snorted. "There is no situation. Your sister was a good wingwoman, but I'm flying solo. Don't need the complication."

I wanted to ask why, because in some ways Jack was very *what you see is what you get*, yet not so much in other ways. For instance, only Max knew everything Jack did for a living. I'd confirmed it with Sophia, who was clueless, even though she'd lived with the guy.

"I feel you. Relationships are on the back burner for me too," I said, "though I'm up for other things." I put the floral blouse back on the rack.

He leaned his tall, athletic frame against a divider that separated the women's section from the men's. "What exactly do you mean by other things?" His expression was suddenly intent.

I shrugged. "I'm not against companionship. Just not interested in a serious relationship."

"Why not? You're passably attractive." He said this all casual-like, as though he was just considering it.

I rolled my eyes. "Thanks for the vote of confidence."

He grinned and tipped up his chin, changing the subject with his next comment. "You going to wear that one pair of pants every day?"

I held up the black slacks. They were cute, in a crepe-like fabric, and lined, which I gave Target bonus points for. I could absolutely rock these for a couple of weeks until I had more options. "Yep. I'll borrow a pair of Sophia's sweatpants for bumming around and pick up a pair of jeans somewhere, but for now, this will do." I twisted my mouth. "I considered leaving a few things behind at my mom's, and now I'm kicking myself for not doing it."

He frowned. "One pair of pants and borrowed sweats isn't enough to get by."

"Course it is. I also have the boxers I stole from you."

He sighed. "Elise, let me buy you more clothes. I own multiple businesses, remember? Paying for a Target shopping spree is nothing."

Jack probably didn't think me incapable the way I'd internalized myself to be over the last few years, but I wanted every one of my actions to speak to independence. So even if he meant well, I wasn't going to take him up on the offer. "Target can get pricey. Having multiple businesses doesn't mean you have money to blow."

"It does, actually."

I looked up abruptly, catching his flat expression. "But you live in a rental inside Max's building."

"Because it's practical. Max can't go a day without seeing me."

I rolled my eyes in disbelief. "You mean the other way around."

He sighed. "We've been in a full bromance for over fifteen years. Happy?"

I smiled. "As long as you admit your love affair."

"The point is," he said, brushing off invisible dust from the divider, "we spend a lot of time together, and living in the same building makes sense. Plus, it's fun."

I nodded thoughtfully. "This is true. Isn't there a third unit?"

"A studio. It's vacant."

I had no interest in moving this close to my sister. I wanted to build a life of my own that I *shared* with my sister. Still... "How much is Max asking for it?"

Jack rattled off a number that was a third higher than what I paid for my last place. Max's building was in a fancy section of San Francisco. Even if the rent was super cheap for Russian Hill, it was still too rich for my blood. "I can't afford that."

"Which is why I haven't suggested it." Jack yawned.

I still wasn't taking him up on his offer, tempting as it was. "Thank you, but I've got this."

Jack stood silently, his green eyes observing me, assessing, as though I were some peculiar specimen.

"What?" I said.

He shrugged, moving his eyes past my face to the other shoppers milling around. "Nothing. You're just—different."

"And awesome, I know." He frowned, and I grinned. "Come on, let's head over there." I pointed at another section. "I need underwear."

"Underwear?" His expression was pure gold.

"Can you handle it?"

He wiped the nervous look off his face and strutted behind me. "I'll even help you pick."

I grabbed a lavender bra that would give my small bust a little boost and tossed it in the basket, ignoring the fact that Jack might be watching. Then I walked a few feet to the underwear section, searching for the exact right pair.

"What do you think of these?" I held up beige granny panties.

His face was horrified. "You're joking."

"Lucky for you, I am." I snickered and put the panties back on the rack.

"Lucky for me?" he said. "You mean lucky for whoever you plan on dating."

Jack moved to a round table with pizza-slice-shaped bins on top and picked through a bunch of thongs. He held up a bedazzled chartreuse pair. "How about this?" His expression was so bland, I thought he might be serious.

"Jackson, that's not my style."

He tossed the panties back in the bin. "Good, because I'd burn them if they made it through the laundry."

"You know," I said, gesturing at the panties he'd just discarded, "women try those on..."

For a moment he didn't seem to get it, and then his eyes widened, and he looked down at his hand.

I laughed, tears coming to my eyes. "Since when did you become squeamish?"

"I blame Max."

Max was more fastidious, though according to Sophia he could be dirty in the bedroom—a piece of information I'd been trying to scrub from my brain ever since she shared it.

I went to a row of panty multipacks and reached for a six-pack of cotton, no-fuss bikinis that were supposed to have minimal panty lines. I tossed them in the basket.

Jack glanced in. "Very practical. Let me know if you ever want to upgrade your underwear game. I'd be happy to donate to the charity."

"So I can wear sexy underwear for my future boyfriends?"

He frowned again. "When you put it like that, maybe you should stick to the big ones..." He started toward the granny panties, and I grabbed his arm.

"Come on," I said, laughing. "Let's check out."

I had just enough in the bank for the black pants, two tops, and new underwear. I'd also grabbed shampoo and conditioner because I was out.

On our way to the exit, my gaze zeroed in on an impulse buy that looked too good to pass up and was sure to annoy Jack. I stopped and held up my hand. "Hang on." I pointed at an apron that said *Hot Stuff Coming Through* and turned to him. "I'm supposed to cook for you in exchange for boarding, right? Well, I need that. Consider it my uniform."

He glanced at the apron. "Is the hot stuff supposed to be you or the food?"

"Me, of course."

He sent me a tired look. "You're only cooking three nights a week."

"You said you wanted to buy me something. This is what you can buy me."

He shook his head and stared at me for a beat, then walked over, grabbed the apron, and headed for the checkout.

Self-checkout, to be exact, which was sexy because it was self-reliant.

And I might have admired his ass in the jeans he was wearing, because he was cute, even if I wasn't interested in dating my new roommate. All guys who shopped patiently with women and bought them ridiculous aprons were cute. This was just fact.

Chapter Seven

Jack

WE RETURNED TO THE APARTMENT, AND ELISE dropped onto the living room couch, toppling Target bags over her lap. She kicked her bare feet up on the coffee table and said, "Home sweet home."

A thrill ran up my spine. For some reason her thinking of my place as her own gave me immense pleasure. Which was weird and unusual.

If my ex, who'd also been my roommate, had put her feet on the coffee table, I'd have been annoyed as hell. She was self-centered and greedy, which was nothing new, because I had a type. She'd also helped herself to my wallet more times than I could count. When she helped herself to *Max's* wallet, that had been the final straw.

Then there was Elise.

Watching Elise economize on the most basic necessities put me in a rage. I could tell she was holding back, not wanting to spend too much. And it made me want to buy her the entire store. Ten stores. A San Francisco city block.

If Elise was going to live with me for the next thirty days, I couldn't get excited over stupid shit like her feeling at home. Needed to keep things distant. And there was no better way to set up barriers than with my next statement. "What's for dinner?"

Her expression was confused.

I tipped my head toward the fridge. "I figure tonight is as good a night as any to set the stage for how things will be moving forward." At her appalled look, I said, "Should have taken me up on the offer to buy you a wardrobe. That kind of gift isn't likely to happen again."

Her mouth closed firmly, and I was pretty sure sparks flew from her eyes. She stood and stomped into the kitchen, brushing past me to the fridge. I'd had the forethought to grab a beer, which I took with me toward the hallway. "I'll be in my office working."

"You mean your bedroom."

"Exactly. Let me know when food's ready."

I settled at my desk and listened to cupboard doors banging and pots clanging. I was ninety-nine percent sure that was for show. No one made that much noise while cooking.

My mouth curved up. Operation *Keep Elise safe but not close* was in full effect and running right on schedule. Though it grated on me when she'd said she wanted to seek companionship while we were out shopping. What exactly had that meant?

A lump lodged in my chest. I didn't want to know.

Hopefully she'd hold off on dating until she moved out, because I didn't think I could remain neutral on that front.

I put on headphones and listened to music while I took care of emails my assistants couldn't address. I had one main assistant for random stuff and four executive assistants who filtered correspondence, not to mention business managers, financial managers, and a couple of chief executive officers for the companies I owned. Environ, the virtual reality company Thalia would be running, was one of them. The idea and programming were mine, but as soon as I came up with the concept and began executing and building business alliances, I stepped back and only interfered if things veered off course. It freed up my time to work on other projects.

Thalia was smart. I had no doubt she could handle the company, but it would take her time to get up to speed.

I sent her an email catching her up on the latest investor. For now, I'd be involved in all the investor relations, but eventually that was something I'd hand off too.

I leaned back and stretched my arms above my head, then rubbed my rumbling belly. It had been almost an hour. Elise must be done by now.

After taking off my headphones and putting my computer in sleep mode, I padded into the kitchen to see what she'd come up with.

The scent of fried food filled the air. Not a bad sign. Not healthy, but whatever—I wasn't picky.

Elise was in the kitchen with her *Hot Stuff Coming Through* apron tied behind her back and her hair pulled into a ponytail. I smiled at how cute she looked.

"Everything going okay in here?" I tried to see around her to the pan on the stove.

She spun, her back to the food and blocking my view, a mischievous look in her eye. "Oh, yes. It's all set." She gestured to the dining table that had only been used by Sophia and her plant designs. It was another one of those pieces of furniture Max had insisted on. At least the couch was useful. This one had been a total waste up until now.

I take that back. Max and I had played beer pong on it once because we were mature like that.

The table was set with plates and utensils and glasses of water. Elise had even folded paper towels in half as napkins. It was...cozy.

A whooshing noise filled my head, and my heart began to race. I hadn't had cozy since my mom died. When I was thirteen.

Irrational fear and anger knotted my stomach. This was the kind of shit I didn't want in my life. "You didn't need to go to the trouble of setting the table."

"Oh, not at all," she said, sashaying over with a covered pot. "Have a seat."

I sank woodenly into the chair, calming my breathing. This was Elise, and she was a wily one. Never had a woman run out on me the morning after sex; usually they were interested in round two. It was my greatest shame that Elise had. Which was why all this was only for show. She wasn't trying to get close. No need to stress.

She set the dish on the table and pulled off the cover to reveal...hashbrowns.

And not just any hashbrowns. They were the rectangular frozen ones I bought and tossed in the toaster oven when I wanted to spruce up my morning breakfast of cereal.

My shoulders relaxed in relief. Elise was being a pain in the ass, nothing more. "Looks delicious."

Picking up a fork, I was about to dig in when she said, "Hang on. There's more." She pulled out a bottle of ketchup she had stashed in her apron pocket and squirted the two hashbrown patties with ketchup in the shape of happy faces. Then she grabbed a jar of sweetened pickles I hadn't noticed on the table, speared one, and shook it off onto the plate.

She stood back and admired her work. "There, now you can eat."

Without batting an eye, I dug into the food, chewing and moaning my delight. I glanced up and caught her frown. "It's delicious. Why don't you join me?"

This was clearly not the reaction she had intended, but she covered it well. "Can't," she said. "I have a date."

Elise untied the apron and set it on the counter, and my hackles rose. Because she'd changed, but it wasn't into her new clothes.

I nearly choked on my food. "Dressed like that?"

She looked down. "What? I thought I did a good job using what I had and borrowing from my sister, *as you suggested*." Her smile was the definition of naughty.

I took a deep breath, having forgotten all about my panic from earlier, and counted to five. "I can see your underwear."

She tugged on the sides of what had to be the smallest skirt ever made. "No you can't. You're just saying that."

I gestured to her legs. "It shows the curves of your thighs."

"Looking at my thighs, are you?"

"Everyone will be. Sophia's much shorter than you, and so are her clothes." Elise was too hot, too sexy. The male vultures of the world would be all over my beautiful room-mate in seconds.

"Which is why," she said while she grabbed the purse I'd finally returned after getting the all-clear from the mold guy, "I suggested going back for my things."

Her things had been bagged and burned, but best not to tell her that.

She headed for the door, and I abruptly stood. "Wait."

She turned. "Yes?"

"What about dinner?"

She bowed and gestured to the table. "It's right there. You never said I had to eat with you. *Byeee*." She pinky-waved.

Chapter Eight

Jack

An hour later, I opened the front door for Max and Sophia. "Did you bring the leftovers?"

Max held up a bag. "Thai from last night."

"That'll do." I'd called and begged Max and Sophia for food because I was still hungry after Elise left—and because I'd been losing my shit when she took off, looking far too beautiful for another man.

"What's going on?" Sophia said. "Is Elise okay?" She glanced around.

"Elise is fine. She went on a date." I studied Sophia. "She didn't say anything to you?"

"No, that rascal. She's been freezing me out of her personal life, and it's pissing me off."

I dished the leftovers onto a platter that barely fit in the microwave and started heating them. Elise had made the hashbrowns to annoy me, but I really hadn't minded. What I had minded was her dressed to impress some other guy.

Though I did need more than hashbrowns to survive. Hence food from Max and Sophia.

I grabbed drinks, and the microwave beeped. We squeezed in at the counter and took turns filling our plates with leftovers.

"So why is Elise living in your apartment?" Max said between bites. "I forgot to ask during the VR tutorial, and I didn't think about it again until Elise was in the room."

Sophia stared, waiting for my answer. It was strange that I knew more about Elise than her sister.

Max was an investor in Environ, so we'd been busy talking shop and hadn't gotten to the personal stuff. "I offered for Elise to live here after I saw her apartment."

Sophia groaned. "It was that bad?"

I gave a noncommittal shrug. I'd promised Elise I wouldn't tell her sister how bad the place was.

"But given your history..." Max said, leaving the thought dangling.

I frowned. "It was one night and no big deal." The lie in that statement tasted like ash on my tongue, but maybe if I said it enough, I'd start to believe it.

Max and Sophia exchanged a look. If Elise were here, we'd be rolling our eyes at their silent communication. Where the hell was she, anyway? It was getting late.

"Not the night you slept with Elise," Max said. "I'm talking about your history of entanglements with roommates."

Damn, I deserved that. "Yeah, that too. I'm not doing that anymore."

"You swear?" Sophia asked.

For a moment, I hesitated. Then I came to my senses. "Swear. No worries there. She's out on a date, remember? About that—how could you let her walk out in your skirt?

You're three inches shorter than her." Elise had looked sexy and beautiful, but I couldn't share those particular thoughts with Max and Sophia.

"Why are you worried about what she's wearing, Jack?" Sophia leaned forward. "Feeling protective? Or something more?"

I looked down at my plate and scraped the last bit of food, avoiding her eyes. "She's your sister; I'm just looking out for her. I can only imagine the thoughts running through her date's mind at that tiny skirt." *Because I was having them too.*

Sophia laughed. "Elise can take care of herself, but I'll text and make sure she's doing okay. Besides, the reason my sister has no clothes and is forced to borrow mine is because of you. She said you burned hers."

How the hell did Elise know that? I needed to give her more credit. "Trust me, it was necessary."

Sophia's mouth twisted, and she eyed me curiously. "I don't understand you two."

I reached for the plates that were now empty and brought them to the sink. "Nothing to understand."

Elise's and my relationship had gotten more complicated with her living here. And her going on dates. And my lingering feelings for her.

"I'm not sure about that," Sophia said. "In any case, I'm upgrading my wardrobe and giving Elise a few things that should fit her better. Don't worry about the skirt. She wore boy-shorts underwear."

I did not need to be thinking about thin pieces of fabric separating Elise's delicate, tender bits from the rest of the world. "I have no idea what boy shorts are, but I'll take your word for it."

Sophia stood and draped her arm over Max's shoulders.

"Send Elise up when you see her. If she's out on a date, that probably won't be until tomorrow, but send her up and I'll have some more clothes for her."

Tomorrow?

A pulse in my temples throbbed. Jealousy tasted bitter, and I was pissed that I knew.

Elise would be out all night, looking gorgeous, with some man she barely knew. How would I know she was safe?

The urge to put a tracker on her came to mind. Then I realized how fucked up that would be and tamped down the desire.

This was going to be a long night.

————

At some point, I'd fallen asleep with my clothes on. But that didn't prevent me from waking immediately at the sound of Elise getting home.

I glanced at my phone. It was midnight, so not too late. I stumbled out of bed and caught her walking down the hallway, head down and yawning.

She finally saw me standing near my door and lurched back in surprise. "Hey. What's going on?"

Clearly, I wasn't keeping my emotions in check. I leaned against my doorframe and forced my limbs to relax. "How was your date?"

"My date?" She looked like a deer caught in the headlights. "Oh, fantastic. He was really...muscular."

Interesting description. "So, not smart?"

"What? No, he was just, you know—he works out."

"Mm-hmm." I glanced down her body. She looked to be all in one piece. "You okay?"

She tilted her head to the side. "Yes, why?"

I'd never worried about a woman out on her own at night, and I suddenly realized I absolutely should have. There were male predators just waiting for a beautiful woman to get within reach. And sleazy men who trolled dating apps. It wasn't safe. Elise could have been hurt or kidnapped.

I puffed out a strained sigh. "Just, you know, be safe out there. Don't hesitate to call me if you get into trouble."

"Trouble?" Her eyes lit with anger. "You don't think I can handle myself? That I'm incompetent?"

"What? No. Nothing like that—"

"Well, I can handle myself, Jackson." She stormed past me and into her room.

I stared at her door in confusion. I'd never been good at reading women, but it seemed I was even worse at reading Elise. "That went well," I murmured and returned to my bedroom.

Elise was home, and she was safe. That was all that mattered.

Chapter Nine

Elise

Last night I'd agreed to go out to dinner with a guy I met on a dating app in order to get out of the house. The key to survival while living with Jack was to not spend too much time together, where we could fight, or worse—where I could experience lingering longing. So when some guy posted a photo of his cute dog, I'd decided to give him a try.

Here was how that went:

1. The guy *didn't* have a dog. False advertisement on his part, though he clearly understood the female psyche and was willing to use our weaknesses against us. Point one to him.
2. He brought a one-gallon bottle of water on the date and refused to drink the restaurant water because "it was contaminated."
3. An hour into dinner, he talked about how we'd celebrate our first anniversary.

Hell to the no.

And then Jack had added insult to injury when I got home and suggested I couldn't handle myself on a date.

Maybe I was overreacting or imagining things, but I was sensitive to people not believing in me. Looking back, it almost seemed like he'd been waiting up for me like a parent.

Jack walked into the kitchen while I was pouring coffee I'd strengthened to the consistency of tar, and when I looked up, my eyes nearly bugged out of my head and the air locked in my chest. All frustration at him from last night dissolved. Because Jack was wearing casual gray sweatpants and—no shirt.

"Hey," he said, yawning and running a hand through adorably rumpled hair. His skin was lightly tanned and smooth, except for light-brown hair on his chest that was less visible from far away but I knew existed because I'd run my fingers through it during our naughty night together.

This here was the problem. Jack was hot, and he was all casual about it. Like it was no big deal.

But it was a *big* deal. Because the casual attitude made him irresistible. So irresistible I'd gone on a date with a guy I should have screened better. In hindsight, if Jack had been worried about my going out last night, his point was valid.

For a second, I considered he might be walking around without his shirt as some form of retaliation for the shitty dinner I'd served. As though he knew my weakness where his body was concerned and wanted to rub it in. But his hair was sticking up every which way, and his sweatpants were rumpled. This was definitely an impromptu hot-guy moment.

He leaned against the kitchen counter, flexing his chest

muscles and making my heart race. "So, about your date. You going out with the guy again?"

"My date?" I said, trying to act smooth while urging the neurons in my brain to fire for things other than his body. "Maybe. It was good—great, actually." I plastered on a fake smile.

He reached for a mug and poured himself coffee, which I didn't think he drank, so that was strange. "Good or great?"

"Huh?" I said, confused by the half-naked man and unusual coffee behavior.

"Your date," he said and glanced over. "You said it was good, then you said it was great. Which was it?"

Crap. If I told Jack the truth, he'd laugh his ass off and tell me *I told you so*. He already had enough ammunition against me: I couldn't pick a proper apartment—or afford one—I wandered around in the middle of the night into strange men's bedrooms—or just his—and now I chose the worst people on dating apps.

It was all there, clear as day: I needed a keeper.

My sister's overprotectiveness told me without words she thought so too. But hearing it from Jack? No—just no.

I was already beholden to Jack for letting me stay the month. He didn't need to know I had terrible taste in men too. "It was great." I smiled, but it was a struggle.

His gaze took in my stiff lips, then slid to my eyes. "Hmmm."

On the surface, one might find Jack absent-minded—unobservant, even. But that man was a hawk. A half-naked hawk with ripped abs and mesmerizing V muscles I didn't remember from our night together.

But that night had been all emotion and feel, and not so much visual because it had been dark. I was seeing more in the kitchen lighting than I had while we were naked together. And it was educational.

Gah! Stop thinking about it.

"Problem?" He leaned against the cabinet and sipped his coffee, biceps bulging. Then he glanced at the coffee and winced before clearing his expression to one of indifference.

Sophia said emotions played out on my face like a book. So I forced my expression to go blank to confuse the lustful thoughts running through my mind. "The date was a solid start. He works out a lot."

Truth. The guy from last night was a gym rat, which was why I'd initially brushed off the water jug. I'd thought it was a part of his health kick. Then I figured out—nope, he was just a hypochondriac.

"He likes dogs," I added. *And freaking lied about having one.*

The dog thing had pissed me off. But what had sealed his coffin was the reference to our future together. After one hour of talking! That part had terrified the hell out of me.

"He's looking for something serious, though," I said before I guzzled the rest of my coffee and set the mug in the dishwasher, ignoring the hot, half-naked guy on my right.

"And that's a problem?" Jack was standing so close I could smell his laundry detergent.

Or what if it was *his* scent and not a detergent I found so delicious? *Crap.*

"Elise?"

I spun and leaned back over the sink, attempting to keep my distance from Jack's pheromones. "What? Oh, yeah. I don't want anything serious." I scurried around him and into the living room.

I sank onto the couch that was soft as a cloud, then

glanced up and attempted to act nonchalant. "You rolling shirtless these days?"

He rubbed a hand over his chest absently. "Haven't done my laundry in a while. The person I hired is slacking." He looked at me pointedly.

Right. Laundry. That was another one of my duties.

"Why?" he asked. "You got a problem with my not wearing a shirt?" I heard a hint of challenge in his tone.

I swallowed. "No problem at all."

"Cool. When no one is around, I like to be comfortable. As long as you don't have a problem with it." He quirked one eyebrow in question.

He's going to dress like this all the time?

"Um, sure. Make yourself at home." Shit, this was not good.

"I'll be home for dinner. Looking forward to what you come up with next. As for the laundry…" he said.

"On it." And boy did I mean that. I needed to get this man a shirt, stat, or there'd be another midnight wandering into his bedroom.

I did not trust myself around Jack. With my luck, I'd sleepwalk right into his bedroom like I had the first time and take care of all the lustful thoughts I was experiencing.

Been there, done that. And this time I couldn't call it an accident.

———

LATER THAT AFTERNOON, I did laundry. Hell yes, I did. This was an emergency. I was hoping Jack wasn't serious about walking around half-naked every day. Time would tell, but at least now he had clean clothes.

Jack had set his laundry basket in the hallway, and I'd

been immediately suspicious. Some of his things looked like he'd grabbed them from the clean pile, but whatever. The man had *extra*-clean clothes now, and I didn't mind doing laundry. It gave me time to listen to the new audiobook from my all-time favorite romance writer. It was a "small town, brother's best friend, neighbor, cowboy, single dad" romance, and I was all in.

I bundled Jack's clean clothes and set them outside his door before heading out. He'd gone into the main office for something, and I didn't feel comfortable going in his bedroom without him here.

Sophia was desperate for help at the shop, so I'd agreed to support her on the weekends. The benefits of a side gig helping my sister? Her shop was just a few blocks from Jack's place, and it helped supplement my non-San Francisco-friendly income at the health department.

I entered Soph's green design store on Polk Street a half hour later and was greeted by fresh air, a shit-ton of plants, and absolute chaos.

"What? No!" Sophia shouted into the phone. "You can't quit!" She caught sight of me, her look wide-eyed and harried.

I set my purse on her desk in the back of the shop and glanced around. There were two other workers here today, a man and a woman, both around my age. The woman's wavy black hair blocked half her face, and her head was tipped down as she jotted notes and spoke into the phone. The guy, meanwhile, wearing khakis and a white buttoned shirt, assisted walk-in customers and what looked like subcontractors.

"Sophia?" I said when she got off the phone. "What happened?"

She pressed her pointer finger between her brows and

closed her eyes. "Two of my employees didn't show, and my new coordinator just quit. Which means I have to hire and train someone all over again."

"Why'd she quit?"

Sophia looked defeated and started shoving folders into her giant mom-purse. "Because one of my best customers is paying her double the salary as a full-time designer for their various estates across the country and in the Bahamas. In short, I lost a designer and a big client."

"Shit. Yeah, that would do it; I'd quit to work in the Bahamas too."

Sophia pouted, but the corners of her mouth pulled back as though she was fighting a smile. "You're not helping."

"But the Bahamas—can you blame the woman?"

My sister sank into her desk chair, cradling her work bag. "No. I'm considering quitting myself."

"You own the shop; you can't quit."

She blew out a harsh breath and her bangs fluttered over her forehead. "Was I wrong to buy this place? I'm over-whelmed."

"You're overwhelmed because new clients are pouring in every day. You'll replace that one client with ten more at the pace your shop is building business."

Sophia sat forward abruptly. "Shit! We have to go." She fumbled with her phone. "We'll be late for an appointment."

In addition to taking calls at the shop, I also joined her for Saturday appointments and typed answers into the spreadsheet she'd designed for new clients while she schmoozed.

I was an upscale typist. And totally okay with it because

Sophia paid well. I figured I owed her too, given all she'd sacrificed for me...

Her teenage years.

Most of her twenties.

All to make sure I could pay my college tuition, minus the loans I'd been forced to take out, because even Soph couldn't cover all of it.

My sister was only four years older than me, but she was smart as hell and extremely maternal. It was like having a second mom, only one who razzed me when I did stupid shit like climbing down the fire escape after I slept with her roommate. She was my sister, my bestie, and sometimes my mom, all rolled into one. Though that last one I'd like her to discard at this stage; one mother was enough.

After two lengthy appointments in Pacific Heights, Soph and I finally made it back to the shop around six.

She kicked off her heels and rubbed her feet. "Thank you for today. I thought we'd never leave that last appointment. Good thing I have my assistant to crack the whip when the clients drag things out."

"Anytime," I said, smiling. "I enjoy keeping rich people in check."

"Speaking of wealthy people, how's my old roomie?" she asked. "You and Jack getting along?"

My heart jumped in my throat. "Shit! I have to get home." I downed a cup of water and slung my purse over my shoulder.

"Hot date?"

My mouth soured just thinking about my date from last night. "Not even close. I make dinner a few times a week for Jack, and I promised I'd make something tonight."

Soph squinted. "What are you talking about? You don't cook."

I grinned mischievously. "I told him, but he didn't believe me. He's letting me live there rent-free in exchange for a few meals and laundry while I search for a better place."

She shook her head. "That's very conniving of you. And probably not so good for Jack once he figures it out."

"Oh, he's figured it out." I laughed. "He doesn't seem to mind my cooking. That man is a garbage disposal. He'll eat anything."

My sister nodded. "Probably why he and Max are such good friends. Max needs someone easygoing to mellow out his uptightness."

I looked up, considering. "Their bromance finally makes sense."

"Why not live in Jack's spare bedroom and pay him rent instead of cooking? Jack didn't go into specifics, but I take it your last place wasn't so great."

Absolute understatement.

I dropped her a comical look. "Me and Jack? We're oil and vinegar." *Except in the bedroom,* I thought. "I prefer the barter system, given my salary limitations and need to save."

Soph sighed. "It's highway robbery how little they pay you at the city for a job that required a master's degree."

"I could make more as a nurse, but halfway through school I realized I preferred sitting behind a computer working on health statistics to drawing blood. Thank you again for talking me into keeping the statistics courses."

"You're welcome. It was probably the first and last time you took my advice."

"How well you know me," I said and raced out of the store. "See you later!"

Chapter Ten

Jack

By the time I got home from a long Saturday at the office, I was tired and hungry.

And my chef was nowhere in sight.

I strolled through the apartment, glancing in Elise's bedroom. Her bed was made, but she was nowhere.

Guess I was fending for myself tonight.

"Hello!" came her voice, followed by the front door slamming closed. "Sorry I'm late. I'll have food ready in just a minute," she called out.

I was taking advantage by asking Elise to cook three meals a week. Or maybe I wasn't. She *was* living here for free. But I could have asked her to do any number of things less personal. Run errands. Buy groceries. Somehow cooking was personal, and I'd wanted it that way. Granted, I'd freaked out seeing how she'd set the table the first time with womanly attention to detail because it had reminded me of my mother, and my knee-jerk reaction was to back away from that intimacy. But dinner with Elise was growing on me.

I changed and walked out to help her. As much as I justified to myself asking her to cook, she worked hard at the health department and supporting her sister, and I was beginning to feel guilty.

It turned out I didn't need to.

Fast-food cartons were strewn on the kitchen counter, and I sniffed the air. "Indian?"

She looked up from where she was setting out utensils. "Is that okay? You said you liked curry. I ran into a place near Soph's shop on my way home. Takeout tonight made the most sense, with both of us working and me getting home late."

"It's great," I said. "I should have messaged and told you not to worry about dinner. I'll reimburse you."

She waved me off. "My treat. I appreciate your letting me stay here."

If my suspicions were right concerning how dire Elise's savings account was, I wasn't okay with her paying for anything. Taking advantage of someone pressed for cash went against every cell in my body.

I sat in one of the barstools, plotting ways to return the cash she'd spent, and in no time we were both scarfing down butter chicken and naan.

She moaned, and a shiver ran down my spine straight to my groin. I stopped chewing and stared at her mouth.

Her plump lips were pressed together, juices making the flesh glisten, and her beautiful face was happily focused on the food in front of her.

So just me thinking about moaning and the bedroom and pleasure. *Fuck*. "This is great," I said, voice tight. "Thanks for picking it up."

"No worries. How was your day?" She looked over eagerly, like she actually cared.

The only women in my life who'd ever cared about how I was doing were my childhood friend, Lizzie, and Elise's sister, Sophia. Lizzie couldn't help herself. She was like a sister and nagged me like one. And Sophia was just a good person. This caring gene must run in the family.

I considered how to answer the question because it was complicated. "Going okay."

She set her fork down, studying me. "Just okay?"

"Thalia's on top of everything with the new company. She's got the employees working on tasks that push the mission forward. She's much better at being a taskmaster than I ever was."

"That's why you hired her, isn't it?" She sipped a glass of water and wiped her mouth with a paper napkin she must have gotten from the Indian place, because I wasn't organized enough to keep that shit around.

"Basically. I'm good at coming up with ideas and bringing in the right people. Not so good at managing them."

"So this is a good thing. Having Thalia run the day-to-day?"

"Mm-hmm."

She set her fork down. "Jackson, why the glum look?"

I shot her a glare, and she smiled. She was killing me with the nickname. "Thalia is a little *too* good at bringing people together. She wants everyone to meet up for drinks in an hour."

Elise scratched her head. "I'm not seeing the problem here."

I shrugged. "I don't like hanging out with strangers."

She squinted. "First of all, you work with these people,

so they're not strangers. Second, how do you meet new people if you don't like being around people you don't know? You've dated because Soph has regaled me with your dating misadventures."

I should have taken offense at that comment, but I couldn't because it was true. "Don't know. Somehow, I manage." I looked over, a thought coming to mind. I hadn't liked Elise going on a date, but maybe it was because I inherently didn't trust men after attending private schools with entitled assholes who treated women like garbage. Maybe if I could find a good guy for Elise, I wouldn't mind her dating someone else. "Why don't you join us?" I said. "I can screen people for you and rule out needy men."

She laughed. "That is tempting," she said, scooping up saag paneer with naan. "Can you really tell just by looking?"

"It's more a vibe," I said, following her move with the bread. "I'm good at reading people. Probably why I don't like hanging out with them. Too many are dicks."

"Don't you have to chat up rich strangers while hanging out with Max and his high-society acquaintances?"

"Yep."

She shook her head. "You're a conundrum, Jackson."

"Thank you."

This back-and-forth felt natural, unfortunately. Good thing I planned to help Elise find a good guy and rule myself out of the equation.

"Okay, well"—she shrugged lightly—"I don't have anything going on tonight. I'll come for a drink or two."

———

Fuck me.

66

This night wasn't going as planned. Men inside this cesspool of a bar where we met up were all over Elise, while she smiled and flirted. To add to my suffering, Thalia was too handsy after getting a drink or two in her.

"Jackson!" Elise called drunkenly, though not too drunk, I noted. Just enough to be beautiful and draw attention. "Meet Brendon," she said and waggled her eyebrows in a suggestive way behind the guy's back.

I already hated him.

But I shook his hand and introduced myself. We chatted for a few minutes, and when he turned to order another drink, I sent Elise a thumbs-down.

She pouted, ditched the guy a short time later, and returned to the table. "Darn, I thought he might be a keeper," she said, sliding into the seat next to me. "Did you see his shoulders?" She made a gesture that mimicked large muscles.

"Didn't notice." I took a sip of my rum and Coke.

Seven of my employees sat around the table, plus Thalia, who'd gone so far as to grab my knee tonight beneath the table when no one was looking. Between Thalia's wandering hands and Elise reeling in men like a fishing pole, I wasn't pleased.

"Jackson, you're too picky," Elise said. "What was wrong with him?"

"Your friend Brendon has a wandering eye."

She glanced at the man, who was currently chatting up another woman. "Shit. He seemed attentive, and he has nice forearms."

I glared. "You said he had nice shoulders."

She blinked innocently. "He has both. Forearms and shoulders are important."

"Sure, as long as you don't mind sharing the forearms and shoulders with other women."

She frowned. "I'm not interested in anyone long term, but yeah, I prefer monogamy."

I was trying to help Elise find someone, so why did it bother me to hear her appreciating another man?

Because I'd had her arms around *me*...

And had kissed and licked her body...

And made her come. That was why.

I was being possessive when I'd never been before.

Her mouth twisted. "I really suck at picking men. You should screen my dating app choices too. I'm especially bad at finding good dates on there."

I squeezed my forehead. "Elise—"

No telling what I would have said if Thalia hadn't grabbed my arm and yanked me closer to her.

"What do you think, Jack? Pub crawl? The gang is talking about heading over to North Beach."

My arm tingled where Thalia gripped it, and not in a positive way. In a bee sting/Taser sort of way. I wasn't attracted to my CEO, and even if I was, there was no way I'd date a subordinate; that shit was messed up. But Thalia wasn't the type to give up easily. Which left me in a bind and reaching for the first solution that came to mind.

I straightened, creating distance between us, and dropped my arm over the back of Elise's chair while she scanned the crowd, presumably scouting out her next target. I frowned, dropped my hand lower around her waist, and tugged her chair closer to mine. "Elise and I should get going."

Elise looked up in surprise. "Huh? I was just about to—"

I didn't wait for her to finish that sentence. She was

probably going to complain about leaving before she could find another man I'd need to kill at a later time.

"My girlfriend is tired." I squeezed Elise's waist firmly, and she squeaked.

Chapter Eleven

Elise

I GAVE THALIA A FAKE SMILE AND YAWNED. "YES—
umm, long day." I didn't know what Jack was up to, calling
me his girlfriend, but I figured I'd go along with it. For now.

But not before I pinched him hard in his muscular
flank. How dare he drop a fake-dating scheme on me
without consulting me first?

He flinched and gave me a closed-mouth grin,
squeezing me tighter.

He knew how I felt about committing to anyone, least of
all him! Even if it was only fake dating.

I'd been a wreck for months after our hookup. So much
so I'd had to leave the country to get back on track via an
internship opportunity that had fallen in my lap at the time.
That was why even faking dating Jack was a dangerous
proposition.

He grabbed my purse and handed it to me, said a hasty
goodbye to the group, who were staring in mild confusion—
probably because Jack had never introduced me as his girl-

friend—then we stumbled out of the glitzy bar on Grant Avenue with him holding my waist and pushing me forward at the same time.

Once outside, I shoved him away. "What was that?"

He scratched his jaw. "Sorry, I panicked."

"What in the world made you panic? You were having a blast vetoing my potential dates." Sadly, Jack proved to possess a discerning eye when it came to other men. He'd point out some awful characteristic about a guy I hadn't noticed, and then that was all I could see. It was super annoying, but likely spared me in the long run.

He grinned. "That *was* fun. But no, that's not why. I was getting vibes from Thalia."

"Oh, that," I said and straightened my purse across my body. "She was all over your tip."

He grimaced. "Do you have to put it like that?"

"She wants a slice of the Jackson salami. Wants to be the bun for your hot dog. Wants to be the ass in the tapping. Wants to slime the banana..."

He winced, and I inwardly smiled. Irritating Jack was the best part of my day.

"Must you put it that way?" He looked green around the gills.

"Am I wrong?"

"No," he said grudgingly and flagged a passing taxi, going old-school instead of using a ride app.

I tucked my hair behind my ear and looked away. "She's wanted you from the start, you know." I glanced over, and he was staring at me in shock. "You didn't know?"

Jack might be able to sniff out the secret desires of my prospective dates, but I was highly attuned to Thalia. She seemed nice enough, and she must be whip-smart or Jack wouldn't have hired her. But that woman had a thing for him. The touching of his arm, the giggles in his bedroom when she'd come over the one time... Oh yeah, she wanted him.

Our past was in the past, but it still irked me to watch another woman get all up in Jack's business.

And I needed to get over that.

There had to be some way to make myself immune to him. Which was why I'd attacked the mission of finding a date tonight like a marauding Viking. Nothing like moving on with someone else to help you forget the past. Granted, having your past help you find someone to move on with was twisted, but what could I say? Jack and I didn't do things the normal way.

That was why I was so upset over the fake-dating thing; it went in the opposite direction of my moving on.

"What are we supposed to do if we're together and we see her? Because given our luck, we'll run into Thalia." The frustration in my voice was clear.

The taxi stopped at the curb, and Jack opened the back door. I scooted in, and he climbed in beside me, man-spreading, with his thigh nearly pressed against mine.

"There's nothing we need to do." His tone was low and intimate now that we were inside the confines of the taxi. He gave the driver directions to our building. "I've made it clear I prefer working with her at the office. I doubt she'll come by the apartment. Besides, now that she knows I have a girlfriend, she won't continue to hit on me."

I snorted. "Sure, she won't."

"What was that?" he asked as a loud horn blared.

"Nothing—" I said, my words cut off as I braced one hand against the side of the car and the other on Jack's toned thigh while the driver made kamikaze moves to get us through downtown traffic. I glanced up, and Jack was watching me. A spark of awareness made my senses snap.

I quickly released my hold and looked out the window, flushed and disconcerted. "I'm just saying, I hate lying. I don't want to have to do it in the future."

"Understood." He looked over sheepishly. "Thanks again for tonight."

I made a disgruntled sound. "That was the one and only time, Jackson. I'm serious."

———

NOT FORTY-EIGHT HOURS later and Jack was on my last nerve, asking me to lie for him again.

He stood in the doorway to my bedroom, where I was eating corn chips and scrolling social media. "I need your help." His wavy hair was extra poofy, as though he'd run his fingers through it a few thousand times, and his face was lightly flushed.

I sat up and brushed crumbs off my chest. "What's up?" Jack was a chill guy. He wasn't the type to embarrass easily or get flustered—the incident with Thalia notwithstanding —so I was concerned.

"There's a society party I need to go to tomorrow night, and Thalia will be there." He squeezed his forehead, let out a deep sigh, then looked straight at me. "There's no way you'd be willing to be my date, is there?"

My jaw dropped. "Are you kidding me?"

He held up his hands. "Hear me out. Thalia thinks you're my girlfriend. I could go by myself, but...well, I think I need more than one time with you to bring the point home that I'm off the market."

"You don't think she believed you the other night?" Of

73

course she hadn't. Or at the very least, she wasn't ready to give him up yet.

He glanced away. "Thing is, she's a shark in business, and I'm getting the sense she might be in dating too."

I sighed. "You're just now figuring that out? I could have told you that the other night. What the hell, Jackson? Tell her you're not interested."

He favored me with a dry look. "She's not the type to take no for an answer. Ask me how I know."

"How do you know?"

He threw up his hands. "Because these women gravitate to me like flies on shit!"

I smiled. It was a funny image, and entirely possible. He was cute and sweet and successful. What wasn't to like? "I see your point. But if you know this, and you're used to women behaving this way, don't you know how to deal with it?"

He crossed his arms. "Clearly not. My track record isn't stellar. I haven't gone out with anyone in over a year because I'm fucking paranoid of repeating past mistakes. I also don't want to hurt Thalia's feelings."

"Back up. Did you just say you haven't dated in *a year*?" That was a long time. And it would mean I had been the last person he'd... No, couldn't be. He'd probably slept with many women since that night. Just not dated them.

He lifted one shoulder. "What can I say? It's been a long dry spell."

He was serious. He hadn't... "Shit." I tipped my head back and stared at the ceiling.

This man... I might kill him. Because I was actually considering this. He was helping me out with a place to stay, and he didn't want to flat-out reject Thalia, his star employee. Pretending to date me would make it so he never had to. "How fancy is the party? You know I don't own any clothes right now."

He fist-pumped the air. "You don't need anything. Tell me your dress and shoe size, and I'll hook you up. Already got your bra size." He tapped his temple.

I closed my eyes. "You looked at my bra size when I we shopped at Target?"

"Hell yes, I did. Fascinating stuff. Still thinking about those granny panties—"

"Stop while you're ahead."

He grinned. "I promise you won't regret this. Keep whatever I buy you and add it to your new wardrobe."

Free clothes? Good quality too. As casual as Jack came across, the guy had excellent taste. He'd pick out better stuff than I ever could.

I was a sad example of the female population. Until now, my fashion sense consisted of sweatshirts and jeans. But I was getting tired of my black pants and Sophia's hand-me-downs. What would it be like to own something nice?

Getting a pretty dress out of the deal *was* a perk. Though the idea of his buying me anything made me uncomfortable. "I don't know."

"Keep in mind," he said, "you'd be doing me a favor, not the other way around. Think of the dress as a uniform, like the apron."

Well, when he put it like that...

"Fine. I'll do it. But this is the last time."

Chapter Twelve

Jack

INVITING ELISE TO THE FORMAL DINNER PARTY tonight was self-serving. I wanted to make it clear to Thalia that I was in a relationship (a fake one, but whatever), as I was a giant neon sign for the wrong women—an issue I was working on. Using Elise as a buffer worked in the interim, and she was good company.

Elise was the last person to get the wrong idea. She only wanted men who weren't interested in anything serious. Something I was curious about, but there'd be time to investigate her rationale later. The last thing I needed was to give Thalia the wrong idea and muddy the waters with my star CEO. Been there, done that with the old roommate and any number of women. Elise was spirited but guileless. That woman didn't want anything from me, which made me want to give her everything.

If there had been one ulterior motive to inviting Elise tonight, it was to get her out of those black pants she wore nearly every day. She'd agreed to keep whatever I bought her, so now was my opportunity to update her wardrobe.

Elise sat on her bed and lifted a long silk dress out of the shopping bag I'd handed her. "Oh my gosh, Jackson!" She clutched the cream dress to her chest. "When I save up more money, I'm going to hire you as my personal shopper. You have the best taste."

There she went with the nickname. Sadly, it was growing on me. Mostly because it sounded like an endearment coming from Elise. "No to the personal shopping, but" —I reached for two more large bags full of clothes in the hallway—"this should tide you over for a while."

She stared in confusion. "But I only needed a dress."

"And pants and every other type of clothing."

She sifted through the shopping bags, then looked at one of the price tags. "Holy shit, Jack. No." She climbed off the bed and shoved the bags at me. "This is too much. The dress, sure, okay, because you need a date tonight. But not the other stuff."

My vision grew hazy, and my teeth clamped shut. "I understand you're independent, but I'm a friend, am I not?" She nodded, seemingly surprised by my frustration. "Then it should be okay for a friend to buy another friend something they need."

She started to speak, and I held up my hand. "I'm done here. Be ready by six."

I left the room and entered my own, with a shocked Elise staring after me.

I closed the door and sank onto the bed. She was right. It was unusual to buy her a wardrobe, but at this point, I didn't care. She could return all of it for something else, but she couldn't give me back the money. That I wouldn't allow.

The way I saw it, I'd made her leave her clothes behind. I was responsible for why she had none.

Conscience cleared, I rose and went to take a shower.

———

I WAITED IN THE KITCHEN, beer in hand, and checked the time. I could be as extroverted as the next guy, but it wasn't my nature. The wining and dining and socializing for work was something I put up with grudgingly. But tonight might not be so bad, having my roommate at my side.

"Elise! Light a fire under it!"

The sound of the Jimmy Choo heels I'd bought her came down the hall. And then I saw her.

The cream color of the dress highlighted her lightly tanned skin, like I'd suspected it would, and the material cut in at all the right places, showing off her gorgeous figure. She was tall and more beautiful than any woman had a right to be.

That kind of beauty made a man stupid.

Holy mother of... Fuck.

I gulped down a swig of beer and set the bottle on the counter, my hand steady even as my heart hammered. "You ready?"

Her hair was pulled back into a low bun at the nape, revealing the slender, elegant lines of her neck. She held up a small purse. "You even bought me a clutch?"

The purse had cost more than the shoes, but it looked nice, and Elise would never know how much I'd spent because there'd been no price tags on those items. Next time, I'd remove the tags from everything.

"Thought you'd need it to hold your"—I gestured absently—"phone." No idea what women kept in their purses, but there seemed to be a never-ending supply of stuff inside.

"But I never dress this nice." She looked sadly at the Cartier clutch. "When will I use it?"

"I'm sure you'll find another reason." I wasn't a big shopper, but apparently, my taste ran expensive. And I liked splurging on Elise without her knowing.

I pocketed my phone and patted my suit jacket to make sure my wallet was inside. "We should get going."

"Wait." She froze on her way to the door. "Are we taking your car?" She looked down at her heels. "I can't walk far in these things. Will we be parking close to the venue?"

"I hired a driver. He's waiting outside."

Her eyes widened. "Waiting? Why didn't you tell me?" she said as she hurried out the door and I locked up. "I would have gotten ready faster."

I peered in disbelief. One thing I'd learned about Elise after living with her for the last week or so was that she cut it close in the time department.

She grinned abashedly. "Fine. I would have taken just as long, but I would have at least tried to hurry."

I reached for her hand and looped it through the crook of my arm.

She looked at me suspiciously.

"Don't worry," I said, staring straight ahead. "Just don't want you to go tumbling down the stairs. That would be messy."

She rolled her eyes. "I need to get used to being close to you if we're going to make our relationship look real."

The idea of being close to Elise had me both thrilled and sweating with anxiety. Any man would want to be next to her. But I needed to stop getting ideas.

I helped her into the luxury SUV, climbed in behind her, then opened a bottled water and passed it over.

She straightened her dress and reached for the water. "Thank you. So, what's the plan for tonight?"

"No plan. Just pretend to like me." I grinned.

She eyed me, her lips pursed as though she was considering it. "That's going to be tough, what with the dapper dark suit look you've got going. You even combed your hair."

I straightened my tie. "I clean up when I need to."

She made a purring sound in the back of her throat while eyeing me, and my heart thudded.

These sexy sounds were the kind of Elise curiosities that could easily drive me crazy.

"So what else do you need from me tonight?" She looked absently out the window at the passing cars as we drove through town.

"Need from you?" I was hung up on the purring. An image of slipping off Elise's silk dress flittered through my mind before I mentally slapped myself. "Eat? Socialize?"

She looked at me, and her face turned pale. "Socialize? With wealthy snobs? I thought I'd just hang with you."

"Not everyone there will be a snob. Some are good people. I'll introduce you to the good ones."

"Okay," she said, but she was biting her lip.

The urge to hold her hand was strong. And this here was the danger in fake dating. It could feel real even if it wasn't.

I tamped down the desire to comfort her and drank my own damn water until we pulled up to the building where the party was being held.

I helped Elise out of the car. "The old Merchants Exchange is one of the few buildings that survived the 1906 earthquake. And the ballroom we're going to inside is named after a prolific architect who designed Hearst Castle."

She looked up at the French Beaux-Arts architecture. "What was the architect's name?"

"Julia Morgan, though she didn't design this property. They named it in honor of her because she was the first licensed female architect in California."

"That is so cool. Gotta love a ladyboss."

We made our way to the carpeted ballroom with hundred-year-old French chandeliers, heavy drapes, and wood paneling. Off the room was a curved bar with art deco details and a massive old fireplace that was no longer in use.

I enjoyed events held in places like this, with history and the echo of the past. Made me wonder if my mother had ever visited some of them.

My dad never sold the apartment where I grew up, and I was glad of it. Most of the memories I had of my mother were in that apartment, and it was comforting to walk the same paths she did. When she died, I'd lost all sense of being grounded. It was likely why I failed at relationships. Max called me "relationship stunted," because the only good ones I'd had were from before my mother's death.

Speaking of... Max was standing halfway across the ballroom with Sophia, sipping red wine and chatting with one of his clients I recognized. Elise and I made our way over, and as we passed, the eyeballs of the men in the room popped out of their heads at my gorgeous date.

Get in line, I thought. Tonight, Elise was all mine. Fake dating had its perks.

Elise nervously checked her dress. She had no idea how beautiful she was.

I leaned closer. "Nothing's out of place. You look..."

She widened her eyes, a little wary, patiently waiting

for the next words to leave my mouth. "What, Jackson?" she said, frustrated when I took too long to finish my thought.

"Nice." She was stunning, gorgeous, and sexy as hell, but I couldn't tell her all that or she'd get the wrong idea.

She rolled her eyes. "Gee, thanks."

Before we could reach Max and Sophia, Thalia popped up out of nowhere a few feet away, wearing a reddish floor-length gown. She was a good-looking woman, only a couple of years older than me, but I didn't find her attractive in a romantic way. That didn't seem to stop the determination in her eyes.

I sighed as Thalia ignored my gorgeous date and made a beeline for my side. "You made it. I've got someone to introduce you to."

I slipped my arm around Elise's waist. "Can it wait? I'd like to get my girlfriend a drink."

Elise stiffened.

I slid my hand to the top of her ass, which had been calling to me in the close-fitting gown since she left the apartment. She was my girlfriend tonight; physical contact was to be expected.

Elise's eyes widened and her lips compressed with a silent message I interpreted as: *What the hell do you think you're doing?*

I leaned down and whispered in her ear, "It's for show."

She whispered back, "You're pushing it, Jackson."

"Drink?" I asked her, loud enough for Thalia to hear in the crowded room.

Elise smiled. "Sounds good. I'll go with you."

I turned to Thalia. "Can we get you anything?"

Her expression was so unabashedly irate, I nearly laughed. Maybe it was the whispering between me and

Elise, or my refusing to leave with Thalia. Whatever it was, Thalia was furious.

"Nothing for me," she said saccharinely. "But Elise should stay behind. I'll entertain her." She smiled—the crinkly-eyed one that opened doors for her in business. The one no one suspected of guile, but that I was beginning to think hid her true feelings.

Meanwhile, Elise dared me to leave her with her glare.

It would be extremely awkward to say no to Thalia after I'd already done so. What harm would come from these two standing together?

Elise was all about independence. This would be good for her. "I'll be right back."

Her gaze narrowed. "Hurry back, sweetie." Then I felt —*and heard*—a loud smack on my ass.

Elise held back a laugh at my incredulous look and flittered her fingers in a wave.

If the ass smack had come from anyone else, I would be annoyed. But what I felt was challenged.

Chapter Thirteen

Elise

JACK AND I NEEDED TO DEVELOP GROUND RULES FOR this fake-dating scheme. His wandering hand had caused all kinds of fluttering, and I didn't need *that* confusion. I was looking for companionship, but not from my roommate! However, I'd gotten great pleasure out of my retaliation and his disgruntled expression after I smacked his butt in front of Thalia.

She was playing it cool, but I had a gut feeling about Thalia, mostly because her eyes roved all over Jack's body when he wasn't looking. Claiming his ass in front of her was to teach him a lesson, and her one too. Thalia needed to know Jack's firm behind belonged to *me*.

Well, not technically. But she didn't know that.

"So," Thalia said casually, eyeing the crowd. "How long have you and Jack been dating? He called you his roommate when he introduced you." She turned and stared at me. "Imagine my surprise when he referred to you as his girl-friend the other night."

"It's new," I said.

Her expression morphed into one of innocence. "Is that why you don't share a bedroom?"

Nailed. Point one to Thalia.

"Exactly," I said cheerily, trying to cover what should have been an obvious flaw in the plan. "I moved in as his roommate, but the attraction couldn't be denied."

She cocked her head to the side, as suspicious of me as I was of her. "I see," she said, and I worried she really did.

I glanced quickly around. *Where the hell is Jack?* People were staring in my and Thalia's direction, which was unnerving. Was my bra showing through the fabric of this expensive gown? It would be just like me to make a fashion faux pas at a ritzy event. The cream color seemed to show every ripple and curve, and I wasn't sure I was pulling it off.

This was why I didn't mess with fancy clothes. They weren't sturdy, even if Jack had paid a fortune.

"Jack needs a strong partner around the businessmen he'll be pitching." Her look was conniving. "Hopefully you're up for fluffing potential investors?"

I choked on an inhalation. "Fluffing?"

The only time I'd heard that term applied was to someone who prepared an erotic actor on a porn set. But that couldn't be what she was referring to.

Thalia shrugged lightly, and her gaze wandered over my shoulder. "The term applies."

Had Thalia just compared me to...someone who gave blow jobs for a living? "The term doesn't apply," I said, but she ignored my comment, a smile filling her face.

I looked back to see Jack making his way over, but I wasn't relieved. I was upset.

Thalia's smile dropped slightly as she scanned my body, making me feel like trash in the designer gown Jack had handpicked. "You were inappropriate earlier, groping Jack. It doesn't look good for him to have a tacky girlfriend. He needs someone with class."

My stomach dropped and my breaths grew shallow. "And your uptight brand is better?" My retort was pure sass, but her comment had hit the mark.

She merely smiled at the same time I felt Jack's arm wrap around my waist. He handed me a glass of white wine, which was my preferred drink when I was feeling fancy. I wasn't sure how he knew that. Though I was beginning to realize Jack could be extremely observant for someone who spent his free time in VR goggles.

My body stiffened, and he glanced down with a questioning look.

"The investors are waiting for you," Thalia said to him. "Don't dawdle."

"What's this about investors?" came a deep voice from behind.

Max and Sophia skirted the couple behind us and made it to our side. My sister was wearing a simple black dress, and Max was decked out in probably the most expensive dark suit in the room.

The man had good taste. He'd also chosen my sister out of all the attractive women in the city throwing their panties at him, so good taste all around.

Jack didn't respond right away. He delivered his next comment to a waiting Thalia. "I'll follow you in just a moment."

Thalia smiled at another guest and walked off, her long maroon gown flowing behind her.

I felt the burn of Sophia's stare on Jack's hand at my waist. Her gaze moved back and forth between it and my face. "What's going on?"

Jack finally let go and stepped back. "Elise, do you mind filling in your sister on our status?" He emphasized the word *status*.

I waved him away dismissively. "Go do businessy things." I considered telling him what Thalia had said, but he already knew she was determined. It was the reason he'd brought me here tonight and why he'd sweetened the deal with new clothes.

Jack strode off, and I might have admired him from behind. The guy was hot in sweatpants and jeans, but something about a handsome, athletic man in a well-fitting suit proved a weakness. It didn't help that he'd combed his unruly brown hair back off his forehead, highlighting high cheekbones and a strong jawline tonight. Good thing he was more of a casual guy, or this masculine display of beauty would be a challenge to ignore.

My sister nudged me in the rib, nearly knocking me off-balance. "Well?"

"Geez, Soph." I rubbed my side. Her elbows were pointy like daggers.

She took in my dress. "You didn't buy that." She plucked the fabric. "This is expensive, and you're as poor as a church mouse."

Nice to have my sister rub in the facts. "Jack bought it."

Sophia's eyes widened, and she glanced at Max, who held an equally surprised expression. "What is going on?" she asked.

"Not what you think," I said. "Jack needed a date tonight, but I have, like, five pieces of clothing in my wardrobe, so he offered to buy me a new dress."

She scowled. "His hand was on you."

I watched Jack meet up with Thalia across the room, noted her possessive touch on his back, and frowned.

"That's because I'm his fake girlfriend. Turns out Thalia is a shark in the dating waters as well as the boardroom. She's been hitting on him left and right." I shrugged. "He says he needs her to run the business, and he thinks this is the easiest way to throw her off without offending her." I pursed my lips. "Not sure a girlfriend will stop that woman, though," I said to myself as much as to them. "She doesn't think I have enough class to date him."

"*What?*" Soph's face turned a scalding shade of red.

I grabbed my sister's hand and tugged it. Hard. "Calm down. You're drawing attention."

But Sophia was looking back, bobbing back and forth like she was ready to brawl. "That bi-otch."

"She kind of is," I said thoughtfully. "I admire her success as a woman in a male-dominated field, and I can't fault her taste in men, but yeah, I could do without the personal insults."

The steam seemed to leave Sophia's body. "It's only for tonight, then? This pretend girlfriend thing?"

"Umm," I said with a shaky smile. "No?"

Max blew out a slow breath and shook his head.

"How long?" Soph said, her voice a little too high.

I twisted my mouth. "We haven't worked out the details." There were a bunch of things we'd failed to work out. Touching rules, how long this thing would go on, etc. Though I suspected it would end as soon as my tenancy did.

Sophia pressed her fingers to her forehead and closed her eyes. "Elise, this is a terrible plan."

"Blame Jackson. It wasn't my idea."

Max's eyebrow quirked. "Jackson?"

I grinned mischievously. "He hates his new nickname."

"Thus you continue calling it," Max surmised.

"You're so smart, Max. I see why Soph keeps you

around. The expensive chocolate you ply her with doesn't hurt either."

Sophia huffed out a breath of exasperation. "I don't keep him around for the chocolate," she said. "He's also very pretty to look at."

Max chuckled, and Sophia flashed him a sweet smile.

"Don't make me hurl," I told them. "I have enough on my plate without your love talk."

"Back to the issue at hand," Sophia said. "Is it a good idea to pretend to date Jack?"

"Nope," I admitted, "but we're in it now."

Max studied me thoughtfully. "It's like watching two trains about to collide. I can't look away. I need to know how this will end." He glanced down at his significantly shorter girlfriend. "We should swing by the apartment more often. I predict fireworks."

"Fireworks?" Sophia said. "This is a shitshow." She turned to me. "Elise, reconsider. Jack is Max's best friend, and I need you two on good terms."

I took a sip of the wine Jack had brought me. "We just need to hang in there long enough for Thalia to get the message she has no chance with Jack."

All three of us looked to where Jack stood with Thalia, talking to a group of finely dressed men and their dates. She was still resting her hand on his back while they spoke to the group.

I cringed.

"Yeah," Sophia said. "She looks real deterred."

Max frowned. "I'll talk to Jack. That can't be good, having to fend off an employee." He shook his head. "He has the worst luck with women."

Chapter Fourteen

Jack

So far, the night had been a success. Environ received one verbal commitment from an investor, and two meetings were scheduled with potential investors who'd gone from cold to warm in interest. Not a done deal, but promising. On top of that, my date was smoking hot, though feisty, and I was enjoying myself, which I rarely did at these events.

Ball attendees had made their way to dining tables positioned off to the side, and we were in the process of tackling the last part of a four-course meal, guests talking animatedly around us.

Elise stared greedily at the limoncello and raspberry mini cake on the plate in front of her. "If this is the type of food I can expect from these things, feel free to bring me to all the parties, Jackson."

I smirked. That was a promise I would hold her to. With Max and Sophia here tonight, along with Elise, it felt more like a fancy get-together than an investor ass-kissing.

"I won't even mind it when Thalia insults me if the food is this good."

I swiveled my head to her. "What did you say?"

Her fork was raised to her mouth, a bite of cake on the end. "Huh?"

"About Thalia?"

She bit the side of her lip and set her fork down. "Nothing. She just, ah...isn't a fan of mine."

The fuck? "Why do you think that?"

Elise picked up her napkin and touched the side of her mouth with it. Her hands were elegant even when they smacked my ass, which I'd deserved. "To summarize, she made it clear I'm not good enough for you."

I snorted. "You're way out of my league."

She blinked, her expression stunned.

I took a bite of cake and looked away. "She's probably jealous. You're breathtaking tonight." I considered that a moment. "Too stunning—a few men here need to watch where their eyes roam."

The warmth of her gaze caressed the side of my face. "Those are heavy compliments, Jackson. You're not going to ask me for anything, are you? Because if clothes and delicacies are involved, I might accept."

I glared, and she smiled.

"As I was saying," I told her, "maybe stay away from lecherous geezers. These rich, old men are crafty."

"Noted," she said. "But the only handsy man so far has been my roommate."

I pointed my dessert fork at her. "That was for show."

"Sure. I believe you," she said, heavy on the sarcasm. She took another bite of dessert. "But your acting didn't pass the test. Thalia isn't buying it. That woman is onto us."

I growled low in my throat. If Thalia hadn't already

brought in new investors and won over my team, I'd consider letting her go. "Let me handle her."

———

Two DAYS LATER, I'd been forced to go commando all day during a very important meeting with community leaders interested in our technology, and I'd felt like a total perv. "Elise!"

I dumped my briefcase on the counter and stormed to her bedroom.

She was sitting with her head against the beige upholstered headboard, hair in a messy bun, long, bared legs crossed at the ankle while she typed on her laptop, wearing nothing but a pair of my boxers and a T-shirt.

I shook my head. Ogling my roommate wasn't the reason I'd hunted her down. "Dammit, Elise, I have no underwear. What happened to doing laundry?"

She looked up sheepishly before her expression turned to one of stubbornness. "That's not my fault. You made me get dressed and go to a party over the weekend, and I didn't have time for laundry. There's a lot of work involved in beautifying oneself. There's the shaving all the bits—"

I flinched.

"—and the polishing of nails and other parts. And makeup, and underwear that doesn't show through fitted silk. And hair! Have you any idea how long it takes to accomplish a natural-looking bun that doesn't stretch my skin like a canvas? And for the record, five-inch heels hurt. So don't give me this 'You didn't do my laundry, woman,' business. I've been busy and I'll get to it when I get to it. Or, you know, you can do a load yourself."

The instinct to tuck tail and hide was powerful.

She returned to her computer and snapped her fingers without looking up. "Close the door behind you."

How had I lost this argument? "Just make sure you get to the laundry." Sophia had tried to school me about heels when she lived here, and like a moron, I hadn't considered that when I bought Elise's outfit. "Sorry about the shoe thing. I should have asked before I bought them."

Her temperament flipped on a dime, and she beamed up at me. "It's fine. They were very pretty."

I narrowed my eyes. Was she playing me? "Speaking of uncomfortable, do you know how awkward it is to wear a suit without underwear? The boys were clacking like castanets."

Elise's eyes widened, and then she bent at the waist and laughed, tipping her laptop onto the mattress. "Really?" She wiped her eyes, because apparently that had brought tears to them.

"Happy my misery makes you laugh," I said, irritated, but my lips might have cracked a fraction into a smile. "It's airy without underwear."

Her gaze slid to my waist, and I felt it in my dick. "You're not helping," I muttered.

She gave her head a quick shake. "Sorry. I guess I can take a break and do a load." She set the laptop aside and slid off the bed. "Just give me an hour or two."

"What about dinner?" I asked.

Her face hardened. "You're pushing it, Jackson."

I held up my hands. "It's in the contract."

She raised her eyebrow. "You mean the invisible contract?"

"The verbal contract."

"Fine," she said and swept past me. "Take your shower, or whatever, and I'll tend to my domestic duties."

Thirty minutes later and showered, I walked out in sweats and a tee to find Elise in the kitchen wearing her *Hot Stuff* apron, which was a good sign. She never made food without wearing that thing.

I sat at the peninsula, and she set a plate in front of me.

"Pizza?" I said, surprised. "And salad?" She'd heated up a frozen pizza and even added additional toppings. But the salad with cut vegetables was the biggest shocker.

This was a huge upgrade from her normal fare. Call me impressed.

Elise busted out a piece of fabric and handed it to me. "Here."

I held it up. "Are these...my boxers?" I glanced at her legs, now covered in the jeans I'd bought her that looked damn good, if I did say so. Her top was something black and stretchy the salesperson had insisted would look nice. And it did. Too nice, because it was hugging her curves in all the right places, drawing my attention and holding it.

And then my body froze. "These aren't... Is this the pair of boxers you were just wearing?"

I'd considered buying her lingerie when I bought her a wardrobe, but figured she'd take it the wrong way and injure me. Now I realized I should have taken the risk.

"Yeah, but don't worry," she said. "I only wore them for an hour or so."

I stared. "Tell me you wore underwear underneath these." The idea of her bare flesh against the boxers was too much. The partial erection I'd had earlier was now at full mast.

She checked the time on her phone. "Of course I was, silly." She took off the apron. "Are we good here?"

I frowned as she rushed to put away dishes she'd used to prepare the food. "Where are you going?"

"Date. Sophia convinced me to try this new app her employees were talking about." She closed the dishwasher and dusted off her hands. "She's worried this fake-dating arrangement will ruin our friendship, and she wants to make sure things stay platonic. Toodles!" She finger-waved and walked out the door before I could catch my breath.

More dating?

It wasn't until she was gone that I realized there was no way she could have done laundry and made dinner in the last thirty minutes. Which meant the only underwear I had for tomorrow were the ones in my hand. The ones that had caressed her long tan legs earlier. And other bits.

Fuck.

Chapter Fifteen

Jack

THE ENTIRE SECOND WEEK OF OUR FOUR-WEEK LIVING arrangement, Elise was driving me absolutely insane. She'd finally washed the laundry, and she'd made a couple of decent meals, as though she was thinking about my cholesterol. And she'd also gone on at least a half a dozen dates.

Some might think she was avoiding me.

The food was no big deal, nor was the laundry. I could do those things just as easily as she could, though for the first time since I was thirteen, a woman had done them for me—and I'd liked it.

I never cared for a woman to do anything for me, but for some reason I liked it so much when Elise did that I'd turned into an asshole and insisted on it. I'd suggested the arrangement so she'd feel comfortable moving in and not paying rent, and here I was demanding she tend to household duties.

The frozen food tasted better when Elise prepared it.

Maybe the extra toppings she put on the cheese pizza or the way she folded the clothes made the difference—I didn't know. But I liked it better. I also liked the way the apartment felt with her in it. Which was why I was about to lose my mind with her going out every night.

And because she was spending her time with other men.

I'd just clicked out of email in my home office when she knocked on my open bedroom door. "Have a minute?"

"Sure, what's up?"

She held up her phone with a spiderweb-cracked screen. I'd been eyeballing that screen, trying to figure out how I could get it replaced without her knowing, but figured that was impossible.

I squinted and finally took in the photo and description on the app she was showing me. Some dude in his early thirties wearing a bandana. "No."

"No?"

"He looks desperate. And douchey." I motioned to my head. "The bandana is a dead giveaway."

"Of what?"

"Perversion."

Elise laughed, seemingly enjoying our battles over whom she should date next. "That's ridiculous."

I shrugged. "I call it like I see it."

She'd been showing me profiles of potential suitors all week, and each time I came up with a different excuse for her to not date them. But some of the men squeaked through when I wasn't around to veto.

She tilted her head while staring at the photo. "You're right. He does look desperate. I bet he's clingy."

"Definitely clingy."

I'd offhandedly asked Sophia if Elise normally went out this much, and she'd shook her head and said, "No, must be because she isn't living at home anymore."

Why living with me brought out her dating bug, I didn't know, but I wasn't happy about it.

Elise sighed and sank onto my mattress while scrolling through her phone.

I eyed her suspiciously. Elise on my mattress wasn't a good image to get in my head.

She looked up. "Are you almost done working? Do you want to grab a beer?"

"At a bar?" I wasn't sure I was up for that, but I'd go if she did. At least there I could cockblock.

She scoffed. "Hell no. The pajamas are on and I'm in for the night. I was thinking from our fridge."

This would be the first time she hadn't gone out in days. "No big date tonight?"

"Nope."

I didn't know why that flippant one-word response made me so damn happy, but I wasn't going to dwell on it.

I stood and gestured for her to go. "After you." Elise sitting on my bed gave me ideas. Not that I needed help in that department. My mind had been wandering there a lot lately.

We headed to the kitchen, and Elise opened the fridge while I sat at the counter. She bent over, putting her ass in my direct line of vision.

I sighed. Her face was scrunched in concentration as she decided between the five different IPAs I kept on hand. She wasn't flirting on purpose; her sexiness was simply a part of her.

Regardless of my attraction to Elise, I wouldn't go there.

I'd screw it up even if I was open to a relationship, which I wasn't. There was a reason my previous relationships had failed, and it wasn't always the women's fault. Some of them had wanted more connection, and that need had shut me down like a Swedish vault. Beyond the superficial gifts and whatnot, I was a trash boyfriend. Which was why I'd been taking a break. I was beginning to feel guilty.

Elise opened a bottle of Anchor Steam—the ale I typically drank—and handed it to me. She pulled out chips and salsa and corn nuts and joined me at the counter with a Sierra Nevada in hand, propping herself on a stool.

The side of my body radiated heat at her nearness. And yet this little moment of domesticity was also peaceful. I liked the companionable crunching, no conversation necessary. Just enjoying each other's company.

She reached for her old-lady word search book—the kind you find on grocery store magazine racks—and started a new page with words related to the Kentucky Derby.

I looked over her shoulder. "Filly—diagonal." I pointed to the spot.

She circled it and crossed it out on the list.

A few minutes later, she was almost finished. I pointed out a few here and there, because I couldn't help myself, but Elise was the master word searcher. She finished those pages in minutes.

She sighed. Then sighed again. She was stuck on "colt." It was always the short ones that got her.

I leaned closer, and she stiffened. Her chest rose and fell more quickly.

Normally, Elise didn't seem all that interested in my presence. At times, she appeared almost indifferent, unless I was getting on her nerves and she called me Jackson. But despite her dating frenzy, in moments like this, I wondered...

"Bottom-right corner, one row up." I stretched, creating distance and acting like our little moment hadn't affected me. It wouldn't be me making a move. I was keeping that shit locked down.

Her phone beeped, and she picked it up. A wide grin split her face.

My Elise Dating Radar went on high alert. Anytime I heard that beep, my heart raced and my head pounded, as though I were having a mild panic attack. I tipped up my chin. "What's up?"

Her eyes sparkled as she stared at the phone. "I snagged a good one."

My jaw clenched. "I thought you were staying in tonight."

"He works in the neighborhood, and he's on his way here." She hopped down from the stool, ignoring my question.

I was the emotionally locked-up one, but here I was, upset that Elise was leaving when we were just getting comfortable. I had no right. But that didn't change my feelings.

I mentally ran though the business establishments close by. "You're going out with a waiter? What happened to me checking your app before you date another loser?"

"This one seems fine. And he's not a waiter; he's a flower deliveryman," she said brightly.

I closed my eyes and sighed. "Yeah, he sounds great."

"Hey." She finally looked at me. "Being a delivery person is a noble profession. What would you do without your delivery people?"

She had me there. I was on a first-name basis with the

delivery woman who worked at the Chinese restaurant down the street. Not that I was deterred. "And that's a criterion for wasting an hour you'll never get back? What will you talk to him about?"

She shrugged. "Plants? Sophia works in green space; I'm sure there are things we can chat about."

"Sophia is a designer with a degree."

Elise frowned. "Don't be an intellectual snob, Jackson. This guy seems hardworking. And he's cute."

I let out a pained sigh.

She checked the time. "He'll be here in five minutes."

The back of my neck prickled. "What? I thought you were joking. He can't really be on his way."

"Well, he is. So you should leave."

Were my eyes popping out of my head? "It's my house!"

She shrugged. "Okay, stay. He and I will leave."

I didn't like that any better. "Forget it. I'm going to my room. But here..." I opened the junk drawer and shoved things around until I found what I was looking for.

Elise stared at the piece of metal I handed her. "A whistle?"

"Blow it if he tries anything." I scratched my head. "Mace would be better, but I don't have that on hand."

She seemed to be holding back a smile. "Do you normally keep mace around?"

"Of course not; I'm a man. I may get hit on, but no woman has overpowered me and taken advantage."

Her face turned bright red, and I realized what I'd said.

She was thinking of that night—the night she'd accidentally gotten into bed with me, and then not-so-accidentally kissed me.

Did she think I hadn't wanted it? That she'd forced me? "Put my number on your speed dial."

She rolled her eyes, her embarrassment fading. "Are you my overprotective older brother now?"

Yeah, right, *older brother*. I tapped my finger on the counter. "Can I trust you with this guy?"

She shook her head slowly as though she couldn't believe my words, and then a knock sounded at the front door.

Her eyes widened, and she pointed to the back of the house. "Go!" At my stubborn glare, she said, "At least wait in your room until we leave. You'll ruin the vibe with your cranky Jackson look."

"He'd deserve it," I muttered. No one called me cranky. I was happy-go-lucky. Except with Elise.

"Now." She pointed again, but I waited until she opened the door, wearing my boxers that were *too sexy to wear in front of other men.*

The guy on the other side had longish dirty-blond hair, was built, and on the taller side. I didn't like him. Not one bit.

Elise looked over her shoulder and saw me standing there, and her eyes flared.

I sullenly walked to my bedroom, where I lay on my bed, face up, staring at the ceiling until I heard Elise rush back to her room. She knocked around for a couple of minutes, possibly changing, and then pounded down the hallway and slammed the front door on her way out.

With the stranger, the fucker.

Fists balled, I closed my eyes, taking in deep breaths. I was pissed, and I had no right to be. I sat up abruptly and grabbed my wallet from the nightstand. I wasn't about to sit around all night. Made me feel like a loser.

Loading a few beers in my arms from the kitchen, I left

the apartment and made my way to Max's place, where I planned to encroach on his and Sophia's couple time.

This whole tantrum I was throwing would be smoother if I had any interest in my own hookups, but I didn't. I was too focused on Elise's dating life.

Chapter Sixteen

Elise

WELL, WONDERS NEVER CEASED. I'D GONE ON A DATE last night, and it had actually gone well.

Conner was super cute and not the least bit clingy. As it turned out, he had bigger aspirations than flower delivery. Even though I'd told Jack I didn't mind the delivery job, it was confusing why a twenty-seven-year-old wouldn't have moved on to something else. Turned out Conner was studying to be a CPA and doing the delivery gig on the side until he finished school. As far as future careers went, that one was stable, if incredibly boring. But to each his own.

I walked down the hallway, balancing a laundry basket on my hip. Jack was at some team meeting and had been gone since early this morning, which had seemed excessive for a weekend afternoon, but he was a bigwig. I supposed it made sense.

He'd been gone a lot lately. I appreciated the alone time, but when he didn't get home until late, it felt off. I'd gotten used to him working in the room across the hall and being here when I returned from dates. The apartment was too quiet when he was gone.

And I was extremely frustrated with myself for thinking so.

Life had been lonelier at the roach apartment, with only my belligerent neighbor for daily interactions, and that was what I'd wanted. So why was I getting attached to my roommate? And Jack, of all people?

No—just *no*.

I entered the living room and turned up the music I streamed through some fancy device Jack had spent twenty minutes patiently explaining. I sang off-key while I folded his surprisingly expensive designer boxer briefs. I did not take him for a fancy guy, but when I looked at the labels of his clothes (they were staring at me, so of course I looked), they were brands I recognized as upscale.

The man was casual with good taste, and apparently spent big bucks on clothes that hugged his...

Stay away from it.

I was trying to block romantic thoughts of Jack from my mind, and I'd succeeded...to some degree. Occasionally. Okay, rarely.

The night we slept together I'd been in some sort of post-sleepwalking stupor. I'd kissed him without thinking. Jack had always been somewhat cranky toward me, so it had taken me by surprise when he returned my kiss. But however murky the physical details of that night were, the emotions remained in Technicolor...

Jack's strong hands had cupped my face, and his eyes were so dark I couldn't make out the green. But the intent behind his gaze had been clear...filled with lust and something decidedly more.

I squeezed my eyes closed, but it didn't matter, because

I could still feel the touch of his lips, cherishing and worshiping me... *Gah, stop thinking about it!*

I sang at the top of my lungs to the chorus of a Taylor Swift song, my voice cracking predictably right as the door-bell rang. Lunging over the laundry basket, I nearly fell in the process of answering the door. But a solicitor was prefer-able to where my thoughts had wandered.

When I looked through the peephole, an older man was standing in front of the door, and he didn't give off a solic-itor vibe. He appeared frail, so not exactly the serial killer type either.

I opened the door without the chain.

The man's eyes widened in surprise. He leaned back and peered at what I imagined was the apartment number beside the door. "I'm looking for Jack..." He glanced past me into the apartment, his brow furrowed. "Haven't been here in a while, and my son's friend recently remodeled the building. Did I stop at the wrong place?"

"No, no, this is it," I said. "Come on in." I stepped aside to let him pass, but Jack's dad looked befuddled—and I was right there with him.

This little old man was Jack's dad?

His hair was wispy, and he had dark circles under his eyes. He was a few inches shorter than Jack and very thin.

"I'm Elise," I said. "His..." *Oh, shit!* Would Jack want me calling myself his girlfriend or his roommate? Shit, *shit!*

Sensing my hesitation, Jack's dad held out his hand. "I'm Tom. It's nice to meet you." He looked around. "Is my son here?"

"He's been working in the office lately."

Tom's chin jerked back. "The office? Really?"

I chuckled. "It's a change, for sure." I made my way into the kitchen and asked Tom to have a seat at the counter.

"Can I get you something to drink?" I opened the fridge and hesitated. "We have beer and...beer. Ah!" I said, happily. "There's also orange juice."

Tom smiled. "I'll take a glass of orange juice if it's not too much trouble."

I poured a glass and set it in front of him. "Did Jack know you were coming?"

"No, I was in the neighborhood and thought I'd swing by. He hasn't returned my calls." The look on Tom's face was more than worry.

I pulled out my phone. "I can try him. See where he is."

Tom waved off my suggestion. "He'll reach out when he's ready."

That was a strange response, but I smiled, suddenly unsure of everything. "Do you live in town?" It would be strange if I hadn't heard about Jack's father or seen him even though he was in town.

Tom took a sip of his juice and set down the glass, nodding. "I'm right over at Fillmore and Sutter."

So not far. And definitely in town.

"How long have you lived with Jack?" Tom said, catching me off guard. But at least this question I could answer easily.

"Just a couple of weeks. It's new."

He nodded. "How did you meet my son?"

Also an easy question to answer. "My sister rented the second bedroom for a while before she started dating Max."

A bright smile lit Tom's face. "I've heard of your sister. Heard Max, my boy, fell hard for her."

I poured myself water and stood at the counter across from Tom. "Max is a lot to put up with," I quipped. "But he keeps up a steady supply of artisan chocolate for my sister, so he has that going for him."

Tom laughed. "That boy has a sweet tooth."

"Did Jack tell you that Max used to sneak down and steal Sophia's gourmet chocolate when she wasn't at home?"

Tom shook his head. "He did not tell me this, but it doesn't surprise me. He and Jack used to clean out my pantry every afternoon. Never saw anything like it. You wouldn't believe the food bill I had back then."

I nodded. "I can envision it. Jack is a garbage disposal. I fed him the worst dinner the other night, and he gobbled it up like it was filet mignon instead of burned beef patties."

Tom laughed, his cheeks turning rosy with mirth. "There were plenty of dinners I made after Jack's mother passed where that kid didn't bat an eye. Overcooked vegetables, oversalted meat—he ate it all." Tom's expression softened into one of sadness. "I think he didn't want to complain. My sweet wife took pity on me early on over my lack of skills in the kitchen, and she did most of the cooking." He shook his head, then looked up and smiled, though the sorrow lingered. "I'm glad Jack has someone now. Glad he's got you in his life."

I'd opened my mouth to correct him when the front door swung wide. I must not have shut it fully.

Jack stepped inside. "Dad? What are you doing here?"

Chapter Seventeen

Jack

WHEN I WALKED INTO THE APARTMENT, IT WAS TO A scene I hadn't expected. My dad and Elise were hanging out in the kitchen, and if I wasn't mistaken, my dad had just called Elise my girlfriend.

"Dad?" I closed the door behind me. "What are you doing here?" The chemo had taken a toll on his body, and he wasn't regaining his health fast enough to my mind. "Is something wrong?"

"Nothing's wrong." He smiled at Elise. "Just getting to know your new girlfriend here."

Elise's eyes widened comically. "I'm not—" she started before I cut her off.

"Sorry I wasn't home when you arrived."

"You know, Jack," my dad said, "you can introduce me to your girlfriends. I don't bite."

My dad's back was to Elise, and she pointed furiously behind him, jabbing at the air and silently cursing me.

I hadn't planned to call Elise my girlfriend in front of

my dad. He'd finished treatment for non-Hodgkin lymphoma a couple of months ago, and I'd been checking on him regularly, but the last couple of weeks had been busy, for lack of a better word, with Elise moving in. Agreeing about her being my girlfriend seemed easier than trying to explain the long story to my sick father. "None of my exes were special enough to introduce you to," I finally said. "Elise is different."

Elise's jaw unhinged.

"Yet you haven't told me about her," my dad said.

"You're meeting her now." I stood beside Elise and wrapped my arm around her waist, hoping she'd relax. "We've known each other for months, but she recently moved in to rent the second bedroom, and things happened from there."

My dad's eyes narrowed. "I see. Well, I like this one. Don't go breaking up with her. You have a pattern, son."

"It's not his fault," Elise said. "He's never dated anyone as good as me."

And there was the real Elise, sassy as ever.

She grinned and pinched my ass where my dad couldn't see, and I pressed my lips together, holding back a smile.

Elise was right. I'd never dated anyone like her—sweet, sassy, smart, and a *smartass*.

She slipped past me. "I'll leave you two to catch up."

Elise walked down the hall to what I assumed was her bedroom, and my dad's mouth twisted. "This one's different."

I set a jug of milk I'd picked up inside the fridge. "Dad, you've never met the women I've dated."

He strummed his fingers along the counter. "I've met a few of them coming and going, like today. They were nice enough. Elise is different."

She also wasn't my real girlfriend, I thought but didn't say. "It's still new, Dad." I poured myself a glass of water. "Try not to get your hopes up."

He frowned. "Why not? You're thirty. Don't you want a nice woman by your side?"

If I said no, it would blow my ruse. "Sure."

His expression grew serious. "Jack..." He hitched his thumb in the direction Elise had gone. "She's a good one. Got a good heart; I can feel it. And she's funny. Don't push her away."

I flinched. My dad was getting more perceptive in his old age. "Noted. Now, how are you feeling?"

He ran his hands down his ribs where there should have been mid-life layering. "Feeling fit. It's why I decided to go out."

My brow furrowed. "The doctor said it's good for you to get out once you're feeling well." I said this more for my benefit than my father's. It was hard to see him moving around while still weak. "Are you sure you don't need the nurse I hired? I can call and have her come back a few times a week."

My father groaned. "Not Nurse Ratched. That woman has balls of steel. She made me the most horrendous food. The kind you give people who are in the hospital on their deathbed."

My stomach dropped. He was joking, but too close to the truth.

He could have died. He still could. The doctors were confident they'd removed the cancer and that he was on the road to recovery, but life was never certain. A part of me had never gotten over the death of my mother when I was thirteen. I couldn't lose my dad too. Other than Max, he was the only family I had left. "It was the nurse's job to help you recover and take care of you. Healthy food never tastes good."

"Healthy is not how I would describe the food Ratched fed me. Gelatinous, sometimes liquidy goo is more accurate. I'd like to live, Jack. Feed me any more of that crap and I'll keel over."

I rubbed my forehead. "Dad, don't joke."

At my tense expression, my father said, "Sorry, son. Truthfully, I'm feeling better. I just need to get back to the gym and regain my athletic body."

I laughed.

"Hey, no laughing. I've lost all this weight; I figure I'll put it back on as muscle this time around."

"You do that. Just make sure you tell me when you're going so I can be there." *And make sure he doesn't hurt himself.*

My dad stood and stretched his back the same way I did. I had few memories of my mother, but her laughing at the two of us doing the same mannerisms was one of my favorites.

"All right, well, I better get going. Don't want to wear myself out with all this activity and not be able to go to the gym to get swell."

I chuckled. "It's *swole*, Dad. You go to the gym to get swole."

"Swell, swole, same thing. Just wait until your old man gets shredded."

I looked at him sideways. "Are you still watching *Real Housewives of Orange County*?"

"Of course I am. Not much else to do while convalescing. Why?"

That explained the vocabulary. "Nothing, just checking."

I walked him to the door and gave him a hug—panicked at how thin he felt in my arms. I started to walk him out when he held up his hand.

"Stay. I've got this."

My dad had his pride. It drove me nuts, but I understood it. "What are you doing tomorrow night? Want to grab dinner?" His appetite was returning, and maybe I could tempt him to eat more with his favorite foods.

"I'm around," my dad said, taking the first step down the stairs. He stopped and looked back. "Just make sure I'm home early. Got a new episode of a show I'm watching..." He scratched his head. "Can't remember the name of it, but the couples introduce each other to their parents the first day they meet." He shook his head and smiled. "Talk about landmines. It's riveting."

I chuckled. "Don't worry. I'll have you back by nine."

Chapter Eighteen

Elise

I LIFTED MY SOCKED FEET ONTO THE COFFEE TABLE THE next morning, wearing Jack's boxers and T-shirt—he bought the extra-soft kind—and watched him putter around the kitchen. I'd taken off to run errands after Jack's dad left yesterday, and when I returned, Jack had holed up in his room for the rest of the night. But I had a lot of questions. I suspected something wasn't right with his dad, and I wasted no time in getting to the point.

"What's going on with your dad?"

He looked up from the giant bowl of cereal he was pouring. "You didn't like my dad? That's a first." He shifted to the side as though he was avoiding something.

"He's sweet," I said. "I liked him a lot. I'm talking about his health."

Jack froze as he reached to put away the cereal in the cupboard. That pause was quick, but I'd caught it. "He's doing well."

"Has he been ill?"

Jack's chest rose and fell on what looked like a sigh, and he finally turned to me. "He was sick, but he's recovering now."

The words seemed to be pulled from somewhere deep, and I did not have a good feeling about this. "How sick?"

He crossed the kitchen and set the cereal bowl on the counter a little too loudly, then pulled out a barstool. "Don't worry about it, Elise."

I stood, walked over, and plopped onto the stool beside him, accidentally bumping his arm while he shoveled food in his mouth. He growled in annoyance. "I *will* worry about it, Jackson. I liked your dad, and he looked frail. What illness did he have?"

He set his spoon down and glared at me. "Will you back off, please?"

I considered it. But Jack was the bottle-it-up-and-suffer-in-silence type. I figured he could stand to unload. And if I was right about this, I didn't think he'd even shared his dad's illness with his best friend. Which seemed off. "No, I won't back off." I stole one of the strawberries he'd added to the top of his cereal.

His eyes delivered an absolute death glare.

I chewed the strawberry and waited.

He picked up his spoon and said, "He had cancer. But it's gone now, and he's getting his energy back."

That was—well, yeah, as bad as I'd suspected. Tom hadn't lost all his hair, but it was thinning in a way that didn't seem natural. "I'm sorry, Jack. Does your dad need anything?"

He mumbled a thank you, then said, "He's fine. I'm taking him out to dinner tonight."

I nodded. "I'll be out tonight too, but I'm serious: let me

know if I can do anything. Drop off groceries—whatever. He's not far from where I work."

He glanced at me. "What do you mean?"

"I mean, I can drop off stuff on my way home from work."

"No, about tonight. Where are you going?"

"Oh, that," I said and brightened. "I have another date with the deliveryman."

Jack's mouth compressed. "Waste of your time." He dug back into his cereal.

I rested my chin on my hand. "This one isn't pressuring me, and I like that."

He studied my face. "He's not good enough for you, Elise."

That was an odd statement, coming from Jackson. "You don't know that. We could be soul mates."

He turned his attention back to his cereal. "He's not your soul mate," he said around a mouthful of food.

I stole another one of his strawberries and stood. "I guess I'll find out."

His devilish green eyes flared. "Dammit, Elise, get your own food."

I hurried away before my grumpy roommate could catch me.

———

Jack

AFTER ELISE strong-armed me into sharing my dad's health situation, a weight lifted. All this time, I'd been keeping what was going on close to my chest, not wanting to make the unimaginable a reality. But now that Elise knew, I felt relieved. And maybe I didn't need to keep it so secret anymore.

I jogged down the stairs of the Victorian and stepped onto the sidewalk. The sidewalks in this part of Russian Hill were steep, so it was either a hike uphill one way or a shuffle downhill the other. But before I could scramble down to my car on the lower end of the block, a movement caught my attention from across the street. My eyebrows rose.

A man was passionately kissing April, the attractive fifty-something wife of a bank executive, in the shadow of her Edwardian row house. And he wasn't her husband.

But the potential infidelity wasn't what had my hackles rising.

I didn't know April or her husband that well. Maybe they were taking a break. He wasn't around nearly as often as April, coming and going in her yoga gear from their four-story home. I could be wrong about the cheating scenario. My blood was boiling for another reason. Because the ass April was gripping belonged to the deliveryman Elise had plans with tonight. He was even wearing the Luscious Stems polo shirt.

"Motherfucker." I stormed up the stairs and into the apartment to Elise's bedroom door, where I knocked a little too hard, feeling my heart pounding from running up three flights. There was no way I'd let Elise date this guy. He was trash.

Only she didn't answer.

I pulled out my phone and hit *call* on her contact.

Straight to voicemail. And what was worse? I could hear her phone ringing in her bedroom. "Elise?"

I knocked twice, and when she didn't answer, I opened the door.

This was the first time I'd stepped inside the second

bedroom since Elise had moved in. Her bed was made, and other than a few pieces of clothing neatly draped over the back of a chair, the room was clean and tidy. The bathroom, on the other hand, was another thing.

Elise's bathroom door hung open, and cosmetics were strewn across the counter. And there was her phone. She must have forgotten it when she went out.

I wouldn't be home until later. What if she went out with this guy before I could reach her?

She'd likely return for her phone before going on the date. I left her a message to call me. There was still time to let her know what I'd discovered.

Twenty minutes later, I pulled into my reserved parking spot in Japantown a block from my dad's place, with still no word from Elise. She hadn't answered my text message or returned my call. Most people had their phones attached to them, but not Elise. She was the only human on the planet who could go without it.

I headed up to my dad's apartment. He owned a two-bedroom, one-bath unit he'd bought with my mom thirty years ago. It was in the heart of this part of the city, and the usual suspects were about: people getting in late afternoon grocery runs at the Friendly Liquor & Market, a new Indian restaurant with a line out the door, and a group of teenagers heading to the movie theater that sprouted up when I was their age.

This part of San Francisco was active without the crazy bustle of Broadway or Lombard. It had been enough activity to keep me entertained when I looked out my bedroom window as a kid, minus the noise to keep me up all night. And yet I'd been begging my dad for years to let me buy him something new.

I wouldn't mind holding on to this place if he moved

somewhere I could keep a closer eye on him. I was thinking a building where we could both live that had accessibility features for when he got older. He wasn't geriatric, but there'd come a day when he was, and seeing him sick these last several months had me stressing about the future.

I unlocked the door and let myself in. "Dad?"

"In the mancave," he called.

A few years ago, my dad had converted my bedroom into a room with a couch and TV. Not a big couch and not a big TV, since the room was small, but it had been a luxury for him.

I unloaded a few groceries he liked that I'd picked up on my way here, then headed toward the back of the house.

"Have a seat," he said and patted the cushion beside him, his attention on the TV. "The shit's about to hit the fan."

The couch was a cross between blue and gray, and overly firm. Then again, Max and the ten grand he'd dropped on the seemingly small, simple one in my apartment had spoiled me in that department.

This was how they got you. You fly coach all your life, but once you travel first class, you're hooked. Anything less feels like torture. But I was determined to remember my roots. Not as though I could easily forget them. My dad clung to this apartment like it was his lifeline.

"How are you feeling?" I asked. "Still up for Italian?" Our favorite Italian hole-in-the-wall was just down the street. They made the best pasta sauce, and if I could bottle it, I'd make a fortune. But the owner refused to give up the recipe. It was that kind of place—super old-school and proud. I made do with delivery once a week instead. Though I hadn't ordered from them since Elise moved in. Had to make her work for her living, after all.

"Whoa!" my dad said and laughed at the people on the screen.

A woman in a bright pink summer dress had just slapped someone I assumed was her fiancé.

"I knew that was coming." My dad shook his head. "Complete dummy, that one. Didn't know when to keep his mouth shut."

"Dad, aren't all these shows predictable? The people are forced into close proximity and break up."

Come to think of it, not much different from my forced situation with Elise.

"Or hook up," my dad said and winked.

I groaned. "We need to get you off reality shows. You're becoming addicted. Your new vernacular is like nails on a chalkboard."

He didn't deny it. "Speaking of close proximity, how's Elise?"

I reached for popcorn from the bowl my dad passed me. I might also have a tendency to eat popcorn and watch trashy television. "Elise is fine."

My dad stared at the side of my face, but I refused to look up and make a bigger deal out of it. "And?"

"And nothing. She's fine."

He moved the bowl out of reach, and I frowned. "I like her, Jack."

"You said that already." I eyeballed the popcorn. Probably shouldn't eat too much before dinner.

"No, Jack, I *really* like her."

I'd never introduced my father to the people I dated. So of course he would be excited to officially meet one.

"The women you go out with don't care about you, and that breaks my heart," he said, surprising me with his words.

Shit, was that a quiver in his voice? "I've never been

interested in anything serious." Maybe he'd get off the subject if he understood how little I was invested in relationships right now.

"But that's the thing; there's something different about Elise. The way you look at her is new. And don't think I missed her pinching your butt."

My arms are long, so I extended one beyond my average-height dad and stole a handful of popcorn. "She's different because she's a pain in the ass." If only my dad knew what she was up to tonight.

He smiled. "Is she a pain? Tell me about it."

I didn't like the look in his eye. "No, I don't think I will. You've got to get off these shows. You're becoming addicted to drama."

He frowned. "Fine, keep it to yourself for now. Just don't hurt my Elise."

I swiveled my head to him. "What the fuck, Dad?"

"Language, Jack."

"*My Elise*? I'm your son!"

"You tend to throw out the good ones," he continued, ignoring the slight he'd delivered with a deft hand to his one and only child. "Like that sweet girl you dated for a couple of months in high school. What was her name?"

"Katrina."

"That's right!"

My high school ex had married a pro football player. Last I heard, she had one kid. Katrina had been too nice, so I'd broken up with her. And okay, my dad had a point. "As I said, I'm not interested in anything serious. Stop pressuring me."

He held up his hands. "No pressure. Just asking you to give Elise a chance. She's the only person you've spent time with who didn't look at you like a meal ticket. I'm proud of what you've accomplished, but it's not good for your love life."

The popcorn turned sour in my stomach. Elise and dating were the last things I wanted to discuss, but it reminded me I had something to do. "Hang on, Dad. I need to send a text."

I pulled out my phone and followed up my last unanswered text message to Elise with another, this one more urgent. Maybe if I stressed the importance, she'd get back to me.

> Jack: Abort mission! Do not go on your date tonight. Caught him making out with the neighbor across the street on my way out this afternoon.

I hit send and stared at my phone to see if she'd message back.

"Who's *Hot Stuff*?" my dad said, making me jump.

"Dad!" He was leaning over, staring at my phone.

He didn't seem the least bit embarrassed by his blatant eavesdropping. It reminded me why I'd moved out years ago.

Thank goodness I had Elise listed on my phone as her favorite apron and not her name. "Just a friend."

His eyes narrowed. "Female friend? You're not cheating on Elise, are you?"

I leaned my head against the back of the couch and covered my eyes. This was going to be a long night.

Chapter Nineteen

Jack

Normally, the homemade stuffed manicotti of my favorite neighborhood eatery put me in a good mood, but not tonight. Because *Hot Stuff* hadn't texted me back, and I was about to lose my mind.

Where the hell was she? Had she ignored my text and gone out with that guy? What was wrong with this woman?

I'd held off running home, but only just, because I didn't want her to think I cared that much. My reconnaissance with Max on the floor above suggested Elise wasn't at his place either. So I stayed behind and watched my dad's new favorite reality show with him, worrying over Elise the entire time and disturbed at how entertaining the show was.

I should tell Elise about it. She'd get a kick out of the family drama in this one...

What was I thinking? Elise wouldn't be around long enough to finish the series with me. Episodes were streaming weekly, and she was moving out in two weeks.

For some reason, that reminder soured my mood further.

I checked a few things around Dad's place—bulbs all looked good and the place was clean, thanks to the cleaners I sent over weekly. Only one bill was sitting on the kitchen table, which I stuffed in my back pocket.

When I couldn't hold out any longer, I said goodbye to my dad and headed home.

All was quiet in the building as I made my way up. I punched in the access code and entered the apartment, hoping to find Elise in my boxers and T-shirt, sitting on the couch with her feet kicked up. A smile pulled at the corners of my mouth. She looked good in my clothes. I should burn hers more often.

But the living room and kitchen were mostly dark, illuminated by the stove light I'd left on. It didn't seem like anyone had been home, and my pulse kicked up a notch. Had something happened to her?

"Elise?"

And then I heard it. The sound of her giggling in her bedroom. I sighed in relief.

Until her giggles were followed by a man's voice. She wouldn't bring that douche here, would she?

My skin prickled and my head pounded. I hated the idea of another man in my home. Especially one who was two-timing Elise.

I stormed to her bedroom and knocked once, then I swung open the door.

Elise turned her pretty head to me, her expression surprised. "Jack? What's wrong?"

My gaze zeroed in on the man sitting casually on her bed. He wore jeans and a black T-shirt, and his hair was slicked back with some kind of ridiculous hair product.

He wasn't touching her—and that was all that saved his ass.

Because it was the delivery fucker.

"Did you get my text?" Heat rose up my neck, and I glared at the guy.

Elise glanced between us, seemingly wondering whom I was talking to. She figured it out because she said, "Oh, um, no. I forgot my phone when I left to help Sophia, and I haven't been back. Why? What happened? Is your dad okay?" She hurried into the bathroom, grabbing the phone where I'd last seen it.

Who the hell went on a date with a stranger and didn't bring their phone? Anything could have happened to her. Did she have no survival skills?

Without giving her a chance to read the text, I stared at the douchebag and said, "He needs to leave. Now."

She glanced at her date, who was beginning to look nervous. Possibly from the flexing I was doing. "Jack, what the hell is wrong with you?" She stepped closer and tried to push me out of the room.

I crossed my arms, not budging.

Elise struck a similar pose. "Just because we live together, that does not give you the right to tell me who I can and cannot see," she said. But I was too busy glaring at Dickhead, who'd had the good sense to stand and move toward the door.

"If you'd read my texts," I said slowly, angrily, "you'd know why this guy must leave. I've sent you six, by the way." I glared at the man who'd stopped a couple of feet from me because I was blocking the door. "He's the neighborhood gigolo. I caught him kissing 2240."

Elise scrunched her nose in confusion. "Twenty-two... Oh, across the street? The well-preserved wife?"

I nodded.

"I'll call you later, Elise," Dickhead said and scurried out of the bedroom after I grudgingly stepped aside.

"Wait!" Elise called after him. "Is that true?"

The front door slammed shut.

He'd reached it fast. Must have run.

I peered down at her, arms still crossed. "You don't believe me?"

Her expression was one of confusion and exasperation. "How do you know it was him?"

"He was wearing his work uniform—the hot-pink Luscious Stems shirt. And I saw his face."

Her chest deflated, and she stepped back and sank onto her bed. "Damn, we had fun tonight. I guess it's back to the drawing board." She pulled out her phone and opened the dating app that was the bane of my existence.

The sound that came out of my throat was more animal than human. "Stop, just stop."

"What are you talking about?" she said, but she was still scrolling through the faces of nameless men.

I grabbed her phone. "Quit dating. At least until you move out."

She stared at me like I'd lost my mind. Which I had. "What are you talking about? What's wrong with me dating?"

"Men are assholes. Except for me."

She just stared, a look of disbelief on her face.

"Fine, sometimes I'm an asshole too...*with you*. Normally, I'm the one getting screwed over."

She rubbed her eyes. "I don't see what this has to do with me. Look, I appreciate you telling me about the delivery guy. He was fun, but not worth *that* particular headache, though I can't fault his taste. Maybe I should date

126

our neighbor and give up on men for a while." She seemed totally serious.

I tipped my head to the side. "Can you do that?"

She pouted. "No. I'm straight as an arrow, and it really sucks because I might have better luck with women."

"I doubt it. Your taste in partners sucks."

She huffed out a gust of air. "And yours doesn't?"

Fuck, she had me there.

Her eyes narrowed, seemingly seeing through me. "You can't honestly expect me to stay home for two weeks."

"Why not?" I said, like it made the most sense in the world.

She compressed her mouth as though she couldn't believe how I was behaving. I couldn't either, so we were on the same page there. "I don't know why you'd want me to not date, but the answer is no, I won't stay home. I need to get out." She said that last part cryptically.

I rubbed my neck. I wasn't making sense—I knew that. But I couldn't seem to help myself. Shit, even my dad was on Elise's side.

None of this made sense. Unless... "You don't need to use apps. I'll take you on dates."

Chapter Twenty

Elise

WHAT WAS UP JACK'S BUTT TONIGHT? HE WAS ACTING like a lunatic. "Why would you take me on dates? I'm not a charity case, Jackson."

"Not charity, just going out together," he said casually, when the notion wasn't the least bit casual.

I must have misunderstood. "Define *dates* and *going out*."

He shrugged. "We'd hang."

"Thanks for the clarity." I rolled my eyes and studied him for a moment. His green gaze showed no signs of scheming, though I suspected there was, in fact, scheming going on. But what would he get out of it? Unless... "Are you expecting sex?"

His eyes widened, a tinge of anger behind them. "Is that what you were doing with the delivery guy when you went on dates?"

I snorted. "He didn't get past first base, but you're acting crazy, so I'm trying to figure out what's going on inside your head."

He seemed relieved by my answer, which was stupid. Why did he care who I hooked up with? "No sex required," he said. "Unless you want to. You might not be able to control yourself."

My face heated. "Are you throwing that night in my face?"

The corner of his mouth tipped up. "Would I do that?"

"Yes!"

"I'm just saying," he said, unfolding his arms and walking toward the living room as though we were discussing the laundry and not negotiating a most disastrous arrangement, "you've got the goods within easy reach, so you might want a piece of this."

My gaze darted down his body. His back was to me, but his ass looked firm in his jeans, and the button-down shirt he was wearing hugged his broad shoulders. I loathed that I noticed. "No, I will not date you, you arrogant jerk."

"Just sex, then?" He sank into one of the barstools, his face expressionless.

I stormed into the kitchen and spun in a circle, forgetting why I'd entered. When I glanced back, he was watching me with a smirk. He knew I was flustered, dammit.

I opened the fridge, pulled out a block of cheese, and took a giant bite.

"No plate?" he said, amused.

"Don't goad me, Jackson, or you won't like the results." I didn't know where this conversation was coming from or what he had up his sleeve, but I was on edge, and I wouldn't be held responsible for my actions if he continued down this path. Between my sister and me, I was the hothead, and Jack knew that. Yet here he was, intentionally riling me.

"Hear me out," he said. "I have a proposition."

"I'm still surviving the last one," I said dryly.

Living with Jack and not thinking about him romantically wasn't easy. Which was why I was determined to go out as much as possible. I'd be curled up killing time on Soph's couch if she wasn't so madly in love with Max and if they weren't so nauseating with their flirtations. More important, I was on a mission to not depend on my sister.

And I didn't want to depend on Jack either. The living situation couldn't be avoided, but I could stay away whenever possible. And here he was, suggesting the opposite.

"You want companionship, and so do I," he said. "Just not with my CEO. Why don't we..." He quirked his brow in a very suggestive, sexy manner I didn't think he meant to look suggestive. Or maybe he did?

My heart fluttered. I took a deep breath, trying to cool the hormone jets. "Jackson, this is another one of your terrible ideas."

"It was good the last time, wasn't it?" The athletic build and posture were all confidence, but the tiniest hint of uncertainty revealed itself in his tone.

I stared in disbelief. "I thought this wouldn't be about sex. And you're choosing now to admit you liked that night?"

He glanced away. "It can be whatever we want it to be. And of course I liked that night, but you ran out on me. What did you expect me to say?"

So his pride had been pricked. But it *had* meant something to him. This was news. Big news. "Fine. What do you propose?" Couldn't hurt to find out what he was thinking, since he was finally being honest. The proposition sounded dangerous, given our history. Also intriguing...

"It would only last the rest of your stay here," he said. "Another two weeks or so."

"You think you'll be able to let me go at the end of two weeks?"

"Hell yes, I will," he said fervently. Which was as reassuring as it was offensive. "The last thing I need is a relationship. And especially not with you," he added.

Ouch. Honesty wasn't all it was cracked up to be. And yet I was still intrigued.

He'd said this wasn't about sex, but that was where my mind went with Jack, and my body liquified at the thought. What were the chances we could have a relationship without ending up in bed?

Jack was Max's best friend. All hell would break loose if we complicated things by hating each other after this so-called *proposition* ended badly. What we shared that night had been intense after my casual, fluffy relationships. Soph had been frustrated with me for months over my neurotic reaction to it. She'd never forgive me if things ended up like the last time.

On the other hand, what Jack and I had wasn't love. We could date and keep each other company—or we could get our fill in the bedroom. Either way, neither of us wanted anything lasting, so we were united on that front.

Unless he'd felt something different that night too...

If we were going to seriously consider this, honesty was the only way. I swallowed, my throat having gone dry at what I was about to admit. "Jack, last time messed me up."

His body tensed, and he studied me for a long beat before his expression softened. "That's because we didn't have rules. We make rules and no one gets hurt."

Jack was a good guy. If he said he wouldn't hurt me, he meant it. "If we do this, it ends when I move out. I have goals, and I'm not ready for a committed relationship."

He crossed his arms thoughtfully. "Agreed."

"Second, you can't tell Max or Sophia. They'd never understand, and Sophia will harass me about it the entire time. You think you can lie to your best friend?"

That got him. He looked off for a moment. "Max doesn't know everything."

Something I was beginning to realize. I was pretty sure Max didn't know about Jack's father and his illness. "You know, I'm starting to understand why you have such terrible luck with women if this is how you set up relationships. Didn't the last one burn your kitchen down after you broke up with her?"

"That's why I decided to give you a shot. You're so obedient."

I laughed—a full belly laugh because he was able to joke at a time like this.

My giggles died down and my eyes narrowed. I had one more condition that wasn't really a condition, but I wanted to see how he'd react. "If I agree...sex is off the table."

"It's on the table. But—" He cut me off when I opened my mouth to argue. "There is no pressure. In other words, it's not a requirement of the arrangement."

I crossed my arms, mimicking his pose, and tapped my finger on the side of my face. He must have liked our first time together or he wouldn't be pushing so hard for sex. Interesting...

There were reasons to not agree to this, but we had something between us. I wasn't sure what I'd call it, but it was there. My subconscious led me to his bedroom that fateful night months ago, and it hadn't been to sleep.

"Enough negotiating," he said. "Are you in or not?"

Jack was very pretty to look at, with those full lips and wide, athletic shoulders. I could stand to get close to him for a couple of weeks. As long as it wasn't *too* close. I'd probably regret this later, but...

"I'm in."

―――――

AFTER OUR CONVERSATION ABOUT "DATING" last night, Jack and I proceeded to take a page from our last book and avoid each other. I didn't hear a peep from him when I left for work this morning. Dating was supposed to make both of us less vulnerable, and yet here I was in a situationship with my roommate and stressing.

Jack and I were experts at keeping our partners at a distance. How exactly would two commitment-phobes come together?

I got off work and went straight to Sophia's shop that afternoon. One of her new coordinators had bailed on her last minute, and she needed help. I had zero skills in design and knew next to nothing about plants, but I could answer the phone and supply Sophia with mochas to keep her going for a couple of hours. In other words, I was her caffeine-run lady.

"Soph, what do you know about Jack's dad?" I said as I typed notes from the calls that had come in. I tried to get as much information from the callers so Sophia was prepared when she called them back.

Her brow was furrowed as she studied a to-do list with at least sixty bullet points. "Jack's dad? I've never met him." She pursed her lips. "Max spent a lot of time at Jack's place in high school, but that's all I know. Why?"

Sophia was confirming my suspicion that Jack hadn't told Max about his father's health problems.

I didn't know why that bothered me, but it just felt wrong. People should rely on their friends and family when deep shit was happening. If Jack hadn't told his best friend about his dad, who was he leaning on during hard times?

"Oh, nothing," I said. "Just wondering where Jack got his penchant for bottling up his emotions."

Sophia looked up. "Does he do that? He always seems easygoing and sweet."

I made a sound in the back of my throat. "That's a ruse. He's very grumpy."

Sophia shifted her mouth in thought. "He's never been grumpy around me, but you do seem to bring it out in him."

"I'm special," I said drolly.

She stared for a long moment, and I grew nervous. Did she suspect something was going on between me and Jack? I had no idea when the dating would begin, but Soph could not find out about our arrangement. That would cause a verbal lashing from my sister I'd never hear the end of.

I ran my tongue over my teeth. "Do I have spinach caught in my tooth or something? Why are you staring?"

"No, I was just wondering if you and Jack are doing okay. You guys aren't fighting, are you?"

We were talking about sleeping together. Or I was talking about sleeping together. Jack was talking about "hanging out" and "going on dates." Meanwhile, all I could think about was whether or not we'd have sex and if that would be a bad thing.

"We're getting along fine," I said. "Though he did kick out my date last night."

"Really? Why would he do that?"

"Jack saw the guy making out with one of our

neighbors."

"No!"

"Yes."

"Well, at least he's looking out for you." She scrutinized her list and crossed off a couple of items. "It makes me feel better that I allowed you to live with him."

I shook my head. "Right, because that's how it happened."

She looked up in annoyance. "Elise Marie..."

I rolled my eyes. Here we went with the sister-mothering.

"The only reason I let you live with Jack is because he's a good guy. You think I'd allow you to stay with some dirtbag?"

"Yes," I said, "because you have no say. But I like to keep the dirtbags to a minimum."

Her cheeks pulled back tightly, and she seemed to be weighing how much to argue with me on this one. "Speaking of dirtbags, who was the neighbor your date hooked up with? Anyone I know?"

We discussed the hot wife across the street and whether she and her husband had split. Neither of us knew.

"I know you can handle yourself," Soph said, "but it makes me feel better knowing Jack is around and keeping an eye on the men you're dating."

I nearly choked on a sip of my chai latte. "A little too much. He's like a testosterone barometer."

"Good," Soph said. "Men are savages."

"Is Max a savage?"

"Only in the bedroom." She winked.

I pretended to gag. "That's disgusting."

Soph thought she could trust Jack. Little did she know, he was the new man in my life.

Chapter Twenty-One

Jack

I WASN'T SURE WHY I HATED BEING IN THE OFFICE, BUT it was the thing I avoided the most in life. As a person who owned three companies (not including the ones I'd sold), that hadn't always been easy.

Once Environ had grown large enough, I hired Thalia to be the one in the office instead of me. But today, I'd dragged my sorry ass out of the house and participated in two team meetings. The growth of our company should have kept my mind occupied, and it did. For a while. Now I had too much time to think about other things. So of course my mind wandered to Elise.

Never thought I'd find myself dating someone just to avoid an aggressive CEO. That was a first.

Who was I kidding? Sure, Thalia was more aggressive than other women, but that wasn't the reason I'd wanted to date Elise. It was merely the excuse I used. I didn't like the idea of Elise with someone else. It just about made my head explode.

I rubbed my temple and closed my eyes, leaning back in the leather chair of the office I used when I came into the building.

Was it such a terrible thing to date Sophia's sister? Elise made me laugh. And she was loyal. Not something you often saw in the crowds Max and I ran in. She'd also been kind to my father—

My shoulders tensed. That there was the problem.

Most people weren't all good or all bad, but I didn't date *sweet* women. Dating women with a few ulterior motives made it easy to end things. But the ramifications of those past relationships had become too burdensome, so I'd stopped engaging. Then I'd grown lonely or possessive— was still trying to figure that one out—and here I was, dating another roommate, which I swore I wouldn't do.

Two weeks wasn't forever, and it would give me someone to take to work functions. So many fucking work functions. Somehow, the timeline made the whole thing palatable.

Thalia stopped at my office door and rapped lightly. "Am I interrupting?"

"Not at all." I rested my elbows on my desk, hands crossed. "What can I do for you?"

She looked down, running her slender fingers along the edge of a yellow folder. She stepped inside the office and approached the floor-to-ceiling view of the Embarcadero instead of my desk. "I was just thinking about our engagement with the Napa investors."

"Oh?" I stood and joined her, peering at the hustle and bustle below. The Environ offices had top-notch views of the bay, and traffic was picking up as people called it a day and got in their exercise along the waterfront. "You don't think they'll come through?"

Her expression remained bland, but I caught her eyes darting to the side for a split second. "I think they will...but they care about appearances."

Where was she going with this? "Our company, along with the others I run, has a pristine reputation."

"They do." She looked over, meeting my eyes. "For now."

I huffed out a breath of amusement. "You're expecting that to change?"

Her gaze was back on the view. "Companies investing hundreds of millions in our technology won't want anything to come between them and the bottom line. These days it can be something wrong with the technology...or a scandal." She wiped an invisible smudge on the glass in front of her—likely causing a bigger smudge.

"Did you hear something?" I turned to her slightly. "Something I should know about?"

She sighed and looked at me. "It's not about what I heard. It's about what I saw. I wouldn't want to pry into anything personal—"

I wasn't so sure about that.

"—but your date at the dinner party the other night was unprofessional."

The collar around my neck grew tight, and I unbuttoned the top. I wasn't a fan of Thalia talking about Elise. "You mean *my girlfriend*. And my girlfriend doesn't need to be professional."

Her gaze narrowed infinitesimally, but I caught it. She looked annoyed. And also perceptive.

Thalia was no joke. Only now, I could honestly say that Elise and I were dating.

When I thought back, my proposal hadn't been romantic, and yet Elise said yes. She'd trusted me. Elise was honest and open, and it made me furious to hear Thalia disparaging her.

"Thalia, stay out of my personal life." My tone was low, a warning.

"All I'm saying, Jack," she continued, ignoring the veiled threat, "is that you and your roommate are different. You're one of the most successful businessmen in San Francisco, and she's—what, a student?"

My chest burned. I hated the insinuation that Elise was *less than*. "She has a master's and is a nurse epidemiologist for the city. She's one of the unnamed public servants helping keep people like you and me safe."

"Right." She sent me a sad little smile. "You see my point, don't you?"

Unbelievable. "Not particularly."

"She doesn't—well, I'm just going to be blunt—she doesn't fit in with your personal and professional trajectory."

Elise shopped at Target and grabbed my ass in front of a roomful of San Francisco's high society. She liked to kick her pretty feet up on my coffee table and eat corn chips like a baseball player with a bag of sunflower seeds. She was feisty, yet could be incredibly kind, like when she'd entertained my father until I got home. And for unknown reasons, she got under my skin. A smile pulled at the corners of my mouth.

"Jack?" Thalia's tone was filled with irritation. She likely thought I wasn't listening to her, and a part of me wasn't.

It was twilight—the view of the Ferry Building and its clock tower indicating the hour—with shades of pastel painting the beige buildings. "You know what they say about opposites." I turned and strode toward the door. I stopped before exiting the office and caught Thalia's open-mouthed look of surprise. "They attract."

I left the building. It was time I got home to my new girlfriend.

Jack: Where are you?

Hot Stuff: Soph's shop. Came here after work to help out.

Jack: Have you eaten dinner? Need any food?

Hot Stuff: Are you trying to woo me?

I grinned.

Jack: Just putting in my boyfriend duties.

Knowing Elise, she'd skipped lunch and only eaten corn chips since breakfast.

Hot Stuff: In that case, yes, please. Bring sustenance. Sophia says she's craving enchiladas with extra cheese. Also, I haven't eaten in a while, and we might have a hangry situation going on.

For some reason, this only made me happy. Because she needed me, and I wanted to take care of her, if only for a short time. Like, say, two weeks.

Jack: Understood. Coming soon.

When I arrived at Sophia's shop, Max was there too—and it was mild mayhem.

"Sophia!" Elise reached for the phone Sophia was holding away from her. "That's my job."

Sophia put her hands on her hips, clutching the receiver. "You're scaring the clients." She turned to Max. "Can you get her a cracker or something? Her blood sugar is low."

Elise's face was bright red, and she had a crazed look in her eyes. She glanced up and saw me.

I lifted the large takeout bag I'd picked up, displaying the goods.

Sophia followed Elise's gaze and let out a deep sigh. "Thank God."

Elise snorted at her sister and speed-walked toward me. "You act as if you don't get hungry," she said to her sister, all casual, but she was reaching for the bag like a vulture.

I held it above my head and turned to the side so the family jewels were less vulnerable in case Elise's knee decided to snap out.

She glared. "Boyfriend, do you have a death wish?"

This nickname I could handle, though even Jackson was growing on me. Because only Elise called me that. "I don't trust you with the food. You won't share."

She pointed at my face. "I cook for you! I share that food."

"You hoard what's in the fridge, and if I accidentally touch something of yours, you snap at me."

"That only happened once."

She'd been saving a bagel she'd picked up from a specialty shop the day before. I knew better, but it had looked delicious, and I might have reached for it. "Once was enough. You almost broke a rib with the elbow jab you delivered."

"Boyfriend?" Sophia said. She stared at Elise. "Why are you calling him *boyfriend*?"

Max walked up to Sophia, staring at us with the same perplexed look.

Shit.

"Shit," Elise muttered, mimicking my thoughts. "Nothing, Soph. It's nothing." She dug her tiny fingers into my side to get me to release my grip on the takeout. It didn't work. "We're still fake dating," Elise said. "It's easier if we play it off all the time."

"How's that easier?" Sophia's look was dubious.

I slipped around Elise's grabby hands and set the food on a clutter-free desk. I hadn't been expecting Max to be here, though I should have. In any case, I'd gotten extra tacos for Elise, so she'd just have to share.

Within seconds, chairs scraped the floor as we pulled them up to the table, and all talking ceased while the food consumption commenced.

But Sophia and Max were exchanging questioning glances and doing the nonverbal communication that drove me and Elise nuts. They didn't seem entirely sure of the situation, but everyone was too hungry to stop shoveling food in their mouths.

"Mmm," Elise said, her expression one of ecstasy. "Jackson, you are an angel."

I bit into my chicken burrito with the works, ignoring her lusty look that had me thinking of other things. "I should have known food would be the way to your heart, since you're so stingy with it."

She smirked. "Don't start with that again. But yes, food is important. Can't you tell by how well I feed you?"

I would not fall for that and admit the quality of her cooking was debatable. I was just happy she *fed me*. It sucked making food for yourself. I much preferred Elise's frozen concoctions.

Sophia pointed a chip at Elise. "Now that you've eaten, go home. It's getting late. I've got this."

Elise frowned. "You're just saying that because I was cranky earlier."

Sophia laughed. "You were, but don't worry, I'm wrapping up and heading home too."

"I'll stay with Sophia," Max said, tossing the final bite of his taco into his mouth.

Elise and I looked at each other, shrugged, then started cleaning up empty food containers. We headed toward the front of the store. "Are you sure?" Elise asked her sister once more, glancing around as though she was afraid to leave Sophia with all the work.

Sophia yawned. "The rest of this can wait until tomorrow. Max and I are right behind you."

With that reassurance, Elise and I headed south on Polk, then cut over into our neighborhood. She was wearing a flared navy skirt with a pinstripe top and a pair of white Adidas sneakers. The skirt and top were basics I recognized from the loot I'd given her, but the sneakers were all Elise and made the outfit. She was professional and fashionable and pretty, and I had the urge to be closer. Which was a strange sensation, but I was rolling with it.

"Let's hold hands," I said. She looked up, comically appalled. I raised my eyebrow. "Get used to it. We're dating."

It was dark out, but I'd swear her cheeks flushed.

"I didn't take you for a hand-holder." She accepted my

hand, and I nearly shivered like a maiden at the pleasure of her touch. And also because her palm was fucking freezing.

"I'm not, but it seemed like a good idea. What in the hell is wrong with your hands? They're ice blocks."

She tried to tug her palm free, but I tightened my grip. "They're always cold. Don't hold my hand if you don't like it."

"I like your cold hands."

She sighed and stopped fighting. After a few more moments, she looped her arm through mine, bringing her body closer. "You like cold hands... How do you feel about cold feet?"

I glanced down. "Huh?"

"My feet are cold too," she said, grinning. "Hey!" Her expression filled with excitement. "Now that you're my boyfriend, does this mean I get foot rubs as well as hand-holding?"

I groaned, but it was halfhearted, because I liked the idea of doing boyfriend things for Elise. Though I'd keep that to myself. "I knew you'd try to take advantage."

Her expression was all innocence. "You call foot rubs taking advantage, yet buying me clothes is acceptable?"

I looked ahead. "Buying you stuff is easy. Wish you'd let me do it more often."

"No."

I glanced at her set chin. "Stubborn."

She peered up, a megawatt smile on her face. "Back to the foot rubs. My dogs are killing me. If I had a real boyfriend, foot rubs would be a requirement."

I stopped her in the middle of the sidewalk and turned her to face me. I tucked a lock of her hair behind her ear and brushed her cheek with the back of my hand. "I *am* your real boyfriend."

Her eyes widened.

Message received.

Sexual tension surrounded us like a San Francisco fog rolling in over the hills, and Elise delicately cleared her throat. "Should we watch TV when we get home?" she said, changing the subject.

It was late and a work night, but I was a night owl, though I didn't think Elise was. "Sure, if you're up for it." We started walking again, and I reached for her hand—and this time, she didn't say anything.

We returned to the apartment a few minutes later and changed into more comfortable clothes before meeting up in the living room.

Elise wore my boxers and T-shirt, and I was in sweatpants and a holey tee. So, our usual uniforms.

She eyed my shirt from her slouched position on the couch. "Don't you think you should put that one out to pasture?"

I looked down and picked at the fabric. The original emblem was faded and cracking in places. "Nope. It's my favorite."

She shook her head. "I can tell."

I sat beside her. Maybe a little too close, because my weight had her tipping against me. Okay, I might have planned that. And she didn't seem to mind.

Elise snuggled up. "You're like an electric blanket."

"Feel free to wrap me around you."

She side-eyed me. "That's naughty, Jackson. Not sure how I feel about having a naughty boyfriend."

I leaned closer, my gaze on her mouth. "You haven't seen naughty, Elise."

Her body jerked lightly, and I glimpsed goosebumps running up her arms.

She lunged for the remote. "What should we watch?" Her focus was on the TV, but the tension lingered.

We surfed Netflix and settled on a political drama that had just released.

Elise yawned and lay on her side, stealthily tucking one of her ice-block feet under my thigh.

She hadn't been lying: those things were as cold as her hands. Had they been this cold the night we slept together? I had no recollection of cold feet, but then again, I'd been busy focusing on other things...

Her small body pressing against mine, waking me. Then her tensing at the realization of where she was.

I rolled over, facing her, and she looked confused for a moment—before she leaned forward and kissed me, seemingly surprising herself as much as me.

Elise had never been just Sophia's sister. She'd always been intriguing and strong in a way I admired. So like any red-blooded man, I'd returned her kiss tenfold... But this was not the time to be thinking of hot sex. Not with her next to me and all too tempting.

I grabbed her foot and started kneading the arch to distract myself. Her feet were bony, with chipped light pink nail polish on her toenails. I smiled. They were cute, just like her.

She looked back, surprised. "Where'd you learn to do that?"

I leaned forward and punched the volume up on the remote a couple notches. "I have skills."

Elise moaned, and the muscles in my arms bunched. Her moan wasn't helping me forget about sex. "That feels so good," she said and burrowed deeper into the couch.

Again, not helping.

We watched the show for a while, and at some point, I

switched to her other foot. When I finally looked down, she'd fallen asleep.

Her hands were tucked under her head and her lips were slightly parted. She looked incredibly beautiful.

I searched the room for a throw blanket. Which, apparently, I didn't own. Somehow Max had failed me on throw blankets. My best-friend home decorator would hear about this.

I was in uncharted territory—taking care of another human who wasn't family. But did I wake Elise and tell her she should go to bed where it was warm?

No, I did not. I hunkered down closer and watched the show, closing my eyes for just a moment...

Chapter Twenty-Two

Elise

I COULDN'T MOVE, COULDN'T TURN OR STRETCH MY legs. I was too tired to wake fully, so I dozed in out of consciousness until I was finally uncomfortable enough to open my eyes. I groggily tried to sit up, but there was a very heavy arm around my waist.

I knew that muscled arm. Knew that soapy male scent. *Jack.*

We'd been watching TV, and then Jackson gifted me with the most incredible foot rub. But what happened after that?

I tried to turn and look at him, and although the couch was as soft as any bed, it wasn't *actually* a bed. With the two of us spooning, I couldn't shift.

So I moved to roll off the couch toward the ground, but I was trapped in the Jack-sized swell his larger body created on the couch.

It didn't help that he was warm and cuddly, and I was freaking tired.

I closed my eyes and enjoyed the moment with Jack off his guard, his body wrapped around mine. The soft sound of his breathing. I could stay like this. Sleep out here for the night. But that would mean waking in his arms, and as tempting as that sounded, I was still getting used to the idea of us dating.

I rolled forward, putting all my weight into it, and tumbled onto the floor between the couch and the coffee table.

When I looked up, Jack was staring, a lock of thick, wavy hair covering one of his eyes, his expression confused.

He blinked and looked around, then yawned. "What time is it?"

I reached over and turned off the TV. Only now the room was totally dark. *Crap.* "I don't know."

He sat up and reached for his phone on the coffee table, tapping the screen to get it to light up. "Three."

Shit! Half the night had passed? I sprang to my feet and ended up stumbling and half falling onto Jack.

His hands were on my hips, steadying me, sending heated zingers spiraling down my belly.

"Sorry," I said and straightened. "We should go to bed."

He stood, yawning again while making a noise of assent. But instead of walking to his bedroom, he stepped back for me to go first.

I stopped in front of him. "Good night." His hair was rumpled and adorable, but his gaze was on my mouth, and the moment grew intimate in the still apartment the way it had earlier in the night.

Clamming up, I turned and hurried to my room. On my way there, I heard him quietly pad into the kitchen and turn off the stove light we left on when we weren't home.

He was shutting down the house, and it was domestic.

Somehow that stupid light made this whole arrangement less casual. He was looking out for me, and no one did that except for Sophia.

———

IT TOOK me forever to fall back asleep, and it seemed like only minutes had passed when my obnoxious alarm went off. I wobbled groggily through my morning routine, grabbing one of my favorite blouses from Jack, along with dark pants. After a few more minutes of applying makeup squint-eyed and detangling my hair, I reached for my work bag and headed to the kitchen.

Would Jack be awake, or would he sleep in? He seemed to be getting up early most mornings instead of the vampiric schedule my sister said he kept. Could be because of his new company and the various meetings he'd been attending lately.

If the city health department wasn't such a bureaucracy, I would have slept in too, but they liked us to clock in and out at the exact same time. No working overtime (that cost them more), and no clocking in late! The exclamation was silent, but I felt it in my soul whenever I saw my boss, who'd taken to casually strolling past the worker-bee cubicles when I was least expecting it.

Only this morning, Jack hadn't slept in. He was standing in the kitchen in a suit and tie, hair lightly damp from a recent shower, and he had his cell phone held to his ear.

"Are you sure you can't make it?" There was a pause in which Jack didn't seem to get the response he wanted. His head dipped and he frowned. "I see. No, no, I'll figure something out."

I dumped my work bag on the counter and went to the pantry. I didn't have time to eat, so I grabbed an instant oatmeal packet for later, along with a hard-boiled egg I'd made a couple of days ago. I glanced over my shoulder to find him texting. "Everything okay?" I turned on the faucet and filled my water bottle.

He looked up. "Uh, yes. It will be."

"What's going on?"

He shook his head. "Just something with my dad."

I turned off the faucet and faced him, arms crossed. "Jackson, are you my boyfriend or not?"

He looked over, adorably perplexed. "Yes?"

"Given that reality, shouldn't you share what's going on with me?" I gave him a pointed look, and here's what was hilarious—I'd never had a boyfriend. Not a real one. I was a commitment-phobe after watching my sister put herself out there with friends and men and repeatedly getting rejected. I'd learned not to follow in those same footsteps. I'd date people for a few weeks here and there, but nothing serious. Yet here I was, schooling Jack.

It was a good thing this was short term, or we'd run into problems once we had to do serious adulting.

He let out a sigh. "My dad's helper is sick. Which wouldn't normally be a problem, but it's been a few days since she was last there, and neither of us have checked on him. She cooks dinner and runs errands, like picking up prescriptions. I'm in meetings all day and can't get there until late." He checked the time again, then rubbed his jaw. "I suppose I could have food delivered and go later tonight. But the prescriptions..."

"I work near him. I'll go after I get off and be there no later than five fifteen. What's the name of the pharmacy?"

He blinked several times. "I can't ask you to do that, Elise."

"You didn't ask me. I want to do it. I like your dad."

He looked uncertain.

I rolled my eyes and shoved my packaged food in my bag. "Text me your dad's address and the pharmacy." I walked past him on my way to the door and smacked his ass, just to jog him out of his stupor.

He frowned, and I smiled.

The ass smack might also be because he looked sexy as hell in his business suit. I liked the dressed-down Jackson, but this worked too.

He was still frowning when I closed the front door. I would definitely pay for that ass smack later.

I'd made my way to the front of the building when I received a text from Jack containing his dad's address and other information.

I was wearing the man down, and it made me uncommonly happy.

Chapter Twenty-Three

Jack

IT WAS INCREDIBLY ODD TO RELY ON SOMEONE FOR help who wasn't a person I paid. When Elise offered to visit my dad, I'd automatically refused, but then she reminded me that she was my girlfriend.

My girlfriend. I'd had them before, but those relationships were different. Max would say I chose the wrong women. In truth, I'd chosen the right women: people who were superficial and allowed me to keep things surface level.

Elise wasn't anything like the women I'd dated in the past, and she reminded me of it this morning by insisting on visiting my father, when none of my exes had known his name. My dad liked Elise, and she had been kind to him. Letting her go made sense.

I shook my head and made my way to my next meeting. This was how you got attached—little kindnesses and building trust—but I couldn't seem to push Elise away.

Max was already on the scene when my mother died, so

he'd been grandfathered in, but anyone else? For over a decade, I'd managed to keep people out. And yet, with Elise, I couldn't. Mostly because she wouldn't let me, but also because I didn't want to keep her away. What I wanted was to hold her close. What the fuck was happening to me?

"Jack?"

I looked up, and Thalia was standing in the meeting room, staring at me staring off at nothing. "Yes?"

"Our new clients arrived. Are you—okay?"

I pulled out a seat at the table and set my laptop down. "Yes, call them in."

I had tech support and engineers who could go over the technical aspects of this project, but if I handled it, I knew it would get done right. My need to control this aspect of the job drove Thalia crazy. She said it made for bad optics to have the owner doing menial tasks.

I didn't care.

The clients walked in, and the meeting went well. We were amassing more investors than anticipated and had the ear of government agencies and a few foreign entities, who wanted to know where and how climate hazards would impact their communities and bottom line. Environ was growing faster than our team of fifteen could handle, and Thalia had left the meeting with a directive to hire experts in other fields to bulk up the program.

This was all good news, but now it was ten at night, and I still hadn't gone to check on my dad.

The doctors were hopeful they'd rid my dad of cancer, but I didn't trust doctors and I didn't trust cancer. The medical staff had said my mom was in remission too, and then the cancer came back a year later and killed her within weeks. Nature could fuck you in a heartbeat and take everything.

I pulled up to the parking space I paid a fortune to reserve a short walk from my dad's apartment and hurried up the stairs to his place, checking the time. It was closer to eleven than I would like.

Elise had stopped by, because she'd texted me when she was on her way to drop off the prescriptions, so at least one person had touched base with him. Even so, my dad hadn't called or replied to my text messages over the last few hours, and I would feel better confirming he was okay.

I let myself into the apartment, expecting things to be quiet and the lights to be dimmed, but that wasn't the case.

"Yes!" came a shout from my dad's mancave, followed by the sound of feminine laughter.

Elise couldn't still be here...

But apparently she was, because a second later she rushed out of my old bedroom, her hair pulled into a low ponytail tilting on one side and mussed. She was wearing a sweatshirt of mine she must have found in one of the closets.

Her eyes widened. "Jackson! Hurry back. The climax is about to begin." She whipped past me and into the kitchen. "I'm getting more popcorn."

Climax? The direction my brain went was obviously not what she was referring to. She must be talking about a TV show.

She dumped kernels into an ancient popcorn maker I didn't know we still had, then grabbed half a stick of butter and placed it in the microwave. She looked over, her brow pinched in frustration. "It's starting—what are you waiting for?"

This was weird. My dad wasn't in distress, my new girlfriend was at my childhood home, and they were—hanging out?

155

I walked to the TV room, following orders.

The same show I'd watched with my dad was on the screen, about the couples introducing their parents on the first date. In this episode, one family was Mormon, and one was Muslim.

My dad looked up, but only briefly—his eyes glued to the television. "Where's Elise? She's about to miss it. Elise!" He fumbled with the remote and paused the show while I sank onto the couch.

Elise came in like a hurricane and half sat on my lap—which I didn't mind—to catch the "climax," spilling popcorn over the side of the bowl as she handed it to my dad.

My dad proceeded to give her a quick recap. "The Muslim mother-in-law's eyes went wide when the Mormon family wore shoes inside their home, but they got over it quickly. The one thing the two families agree on is no sex before marriage. They might have more in common than they think."

Strangely, the show was engaging, particularly while listening to my dad and Elise's commentary.

"No!" Elise shouted.

My dad covered his eyes. "I can't watch."

Elise reached for my dad's hand. "Tom, we do this together or we don't do it at all."

"Right you are," my dad said.

Was this the *Titanic* sinking or a reality show? I reached for the popcorn, amused at the two of them.

My dad had decent color tonight, though he was wearing a blanket over his legs that Elise adjusted when it started to slip. She'd also brought him a glass of water when he paused the show and got up to use the bathroom. They acted like they'd known each other for years.

I tipped my chin up at Elise while my dad was in the bathroom. "You decided to stay?"

"Tom got me sucked into this show. I've watched four episodes straight. I might stroke out from all the secondhand embarrassment and drama."

"Is that the reason for the crazed look in your eyes?"

She patted her face, then seemed to come to her senses. "Jackson, this show is addictive. How can you not like it?"

"Oh, I like it. My dad got me hooked on it the last time I was here." I didn't mention that I had planned to tell her about the show. "Just curious how you two ended up hanging out for several hours."

"Well," she started, "I was hungry, so I grabbed takeout for the two of us. I figured we could eat together and then I'd go home. But then your dad gave me a tour of your old bedroom and photos—"

"Photos?" My voice took on an unusually high pitch. "What photos?"

She smiled devilishly. "You as a naked baby...another after you'd dressed yourself for kindergarten. Then one where you were taking a girl to an eighth-grade dance. What was with the peach fuzz on your lip? Didn't you think to shave that caterpillar? And was that girl six feet tall? You were, like, a foot shorter."

I closed my eyes briefly. "My God, he showed you everything."

"He did. Tom and I are besties now." She looked up, scrunching her face. "I should introduce him to my mom. Not as a dating thing, but as a parents-who-could-hang kind of thing. I think they'd get along."

"Wonderful," I said dryly. "We could bring Kitty and Karl along and make it a parental party."

"Excellent idea!"

"I was joking."

Her brow furrowed. "Hasn't your dad met Max's parents before?"

I thought back. "Max's family had a driver who took Max everywhere until we could drive. And my dad worked a lot—so no, I don't think their paths ever crossed. Max's parents were busier before they lost most of their fortune."

She rested her chin on her hand. "Right, all the hoopla about Max's family fortune being squandered due to poor investing."

Sophia must have caught Elise up on Max's family drama.

I shrugged. "They didn't listen to Max when he told them not to invest."

"Curious."

"His parents not listening to him?"

"No, the part about you guys being best friends and your parents never meeting."

My dad walked in, un-paused the show, and sank into his recliner. The man was so excited, he'd taken the remote into the bathroom with him.

I wasn't as fastidious as Max in the cleanliness department, but even that curled my nose. "Dad, maybe we should wipe down the remote."

He waved me off. "I left it on the counter and didn't touch it until my hands were clean."

So he may be using pop vernacular, but he hadn't lost all dignity due to reality TV.

We finished the rest of the episode in relative silence, except for my dad and Elise's dueling commentary.

"He did not just say that," Elise said.

My dad shook his head. "Doghouse for that boy."

I found their camaraderie more entertaining than the

show and had to put effort into watching the TV and not the two of them.

When the episode was finally over, I stood. "We should get going, Elise."

She checked her phone and sighed. "Yeah, probably a good idea." She leaned over and hugged my dad. "Same time next week?"

"You better believe it." My dad grinned, thrilled at his new friend. You'd think he'd won the lottery, he was beaming so wide.

After locking up the place, I walked Elise to my car and opened the door. She yawned and sank into the passenger seat.

On our way back to the apartment, I glanced over. "Thank you for taking care of my dad."

She tilted her head against the passenger seat headrest, and another yawn escaped. "It was no trouble. Anytime."

Once we got back to our place, Elise went into autopilot. She toed off her shoes in the entry, dumped her purse onto the counter, and walked to her bedroom, eyes half-lidded. "Night, night, Jackson."

She was cute when she was tired. I grinned and locked the front door, then grabbed a glass of water before heading to bed. I'd just checked my phone alarm and closed my eyes when I felt a dip in the mattress.

A second later, a small, warm body pressed against mine.

Am I dreaming?

I carefully rolled over to find Elise curled on her side, her hands tucked under her cheek, sound asleep. She'd sleepwalked into my bedroom.

The first time Elise had done this, it ended in a one-night stand, after which she ditched me by leaving via the

JULES BARNARD

fire escape from Sophia's then-bedroom across the hall. I'd learned later that Elise was a notorious sleepwalker. But even though she'd wandered into my room asleep, she hadn't remained that way. She'd woken, realized where she was, and then kissed me. I'd been lusting after Elise for months by that point. Her kiss had been all the encouragement I needed to reciprocate.

I brushed a lock of hair from her eye, wondering if she'd wake the way she had that night and how I'd respond. Probably the same—eagerly.

But tonight, she only slept. And was snuggly. She scooched closer at my touch.

This should be awkward, but it wasn't. It was amazing.

I stared up at the ceiling and sighed. How was I going to keep up my end of the bargain and let Elise go in a week? I was falling for her, and I didn't want her to leave.

On that thought, I pulled her closer and breathed in her scent, soaking it in while I could and hoping it wouldn't be the last time.

———

WHEN MY ALARM went off at seven, I woke to déjà vu of the night Elise and I had slept together months ago. Because she was gone.

Had I dreamed she'd come into my bed last night? The tent I was pitching this morning said she'd been here.

I picked up the pillow she'd laid her head on and smelled it: buttercream and strawberries and something floral. The scent did nothing to chill my erection. Elise had definitely been here.

My chest tightened. Had she left without saying goodbye?

160

I reached for my phone and saw a note scribbled on the back of a grocery receipt.

Sorry about the sleepwalking! Geez! My subconscious likes your bed. I'll make up for it tonight with dinner. Make sure you come home hungry.
    Elise

Elise's handwriting was neat and elegant. I don't know what I expected, but not something so pretty.

Dinner? More frozen food? Fast food? Didn't matter; I was game.

I rushed through my morning routine and was at my bedroom desk by eight, making phone calls and emailing my assistant to book a helicopter to Napa for me and Thalia a week from today for an investor lunch. By the time I checked the time, it was only three in the afternoon. Fuck, this day was dragging.

Elise should be home around six, which meant I had several hours until I saw her. I decided to catch up with Max.

> Jack: Have you heard from Lizzie? She was text-harassing me for two months straight, but I haven't heard from her in a couple of weeks.

> Max: Had lunch with her about a month ago. She traveled to the East Coast for work, but she's back now.

I'd met Lizzie at the same time I met Max, probably because she'd been Max's friend first. Lizzie came from the same high society Max did, but like Max, she wasn't anything like the people in their world. Lizzie was open, inclusive, and warm, and extremely fun to be around.

I'd spent quite a bit of time around Max's parents and their friends, but it wasn't until I sold my first company at the ripe age of nineteen for a fortune that high society gave me a second glance. Suddenly, I had value. Suddenly, they wanted to do business with me. Suddenly, they wanted to introduce me to this person or that person in exchange for an early in on my next project. Max's parents were decent people underneath it all, but the others... Most were fuckers.

I typed out a text to Lizzie.

> Jack: Where are you? Where's my daily
> dose of ridicule?

Almost immediately, I received a response.

> Lizzie: Calm down. I'm dealing with client
> drama. I don't have time to send you reels.

Lizzie's harassment usually came in the form of funny animal reels she sent daily. One of a chicken chasing a dog or a dog stomping on a pig to get it to play. Now that I thought about it, this was probably her way of saying, "Come hang out."

> Jack: What happened to friends before
> work?

> Lizzie: Was that ever a thing?

> Jack: I just made it one.

> Lizzie: (eye-roll emoji) Says the guy who's running multiple companies and shows up to lunch in sweatpants—when he bothers to show up.

> Jack: I've stepped it up. I wear jeans now.

> Lizzie: Are you and Max in cahoots? He just texted me. I hear nothing from you knuckleheads for weeks, and suddenly everyone wants a piece of me.

I chuckled. Same old Lizzie.

> Jack: Beer night?

> Lizzie: Sure, I could use it.

We moved to a group text with Max and discussed dates while bickering about availability, because when Max and I were free, Lizzie wasn't, and she liked to point out how difficult we were. We finally settled on a time and day, and the text thread went silent.

When I glanced at the time again, it was only half past three. I groaned, unable to focus.

Instead of hanging around the house pretending to work and waiting for Elise to get home, I changed into running shoes. I had a lot of pent-up energy that had begun this morning after waking fully aroused. Running up and down Russian Hill a few dozen times should help cool the jets.

Chapter Twenty-Four

Elise

I set a ridiculously expensive cut of meat in the pan while talking to Soph on the phone, and it started to sizzle.

Was the temperature too hot?

I checked the stovetop, but according to the filet mignon directions on YouTube (the font of gourmet cooking), I was preparing it correctly.

Sophia squawked through my earbuds. "You're cooking? I thought you were joking when you said you cooked for Jack. Do you even know how?"

"I can use an oven, Soph. And I'm a master at the microwave." I thought back. "I also make killer fresh popcorn."

"Since when?"

The popcorn was a recent development, and Jack's dad might have had to shout out pointers to me from the TV room, but it came out amazing. "Since this week. Anyway, why are you bitching? You're no chef. It's a lucky thing you nabbed a billionaire who likes to make you food. Besides, is it any surprise that neither of us can cook? That was the one thing Mom did well."

Mom was good at preparing food. She even washed and put away dishes. It was the insane collection of random shit that had been the brunt of her hoarding problem. Until she had a stroke several months ago and finally got therapy for a fifteen-year-old trauma. Our mom was doing much better now—not perfect, but better. Sophia and I occasionally saw her struggling with the desire to hold on to something, but her house was no longer a hazard zone. And she sounded happy when I called her these days, which made me happy.

"Exactly," Sophia said, "so why are you going to this length if you and Jack are only fake dating?" She sounded suspicious.

If I told her the truth, and that Jack and I were dating for real, though only for the next week or so, I'd have even bigger issues. I liked Jack, and waking in his arms had been incredible, if accidental. I wanted to do something nice for him. But I kept the real reason for the food prep to something Sophia would not freak out over. Well, not as much, anyway. "I might have fallen asleep in Jack's bed last night."

"*What?*" Rustling and scratching sounds came through the earbuds, as though she'd dropped her phone, then, "Elise Marie!"

"Look, Soph, the cat's out of the bag. Jack and I have already slept together. Figuratively and literally. Is it such a big deal if we shared a bed?" This was all bravado on my part, because waking up in Jack's arms had been startling. And also the most natural thing in the world. But I'd worry about that salient fact later. "I sleepwalk; what else is new? Your old roommate is used to it by now."

"Only because the last time you also landed on his penis and boned! I can't take you anywhere!"

"Boned? Really, Soph? Show some class."

We'd *so* boned. I'd boned that man good. And had been thinking of doing it again this morning when I took in his bared, muscular chest. It had required an enormous amount of mental fortitude to drag my tired ass out of Jack's arms.

"In any case," I said, "I'm cooking to make up for the sleepwalking and late-night intrusion. It's all good. Jackson loves my cooking."

"Jack would eat crocodile meat if you put it in front of him."

Ew. "Isn't that supposed to taste like fish?"

"I don't know. But you understand my point. He's not picky."

"Which works to my advantage, because I might have just burned this astronomically expensive steak. Gotta go!"

"Don't you dare hang—"

I hung up. I wasn't joking. The meat was looking crispy. I flipped it over and turned off the heat, then heard him entering the apartment.

He walked into the kitchen, his T-shirt drenched with sweat, clad in running shorts and shoes.

"What's that smell?" he said, setting down a bag of groceries on the counter a few feet away.

I punched my fists to my hips. "Is that how you greet your chef who's been slaving for hours to prepare you a home-cooked meal?"

He delivered a disbelieving look. "Has there been cooking involved? Your form of meal prep is heating up frozen items in the microwave." He walked over, and I noticed his damp T-shirt sticking to the chest muscles I'd investigated thoroughly this morning. Then he leaned over my shoulder and pulled the top off the pan. "Hey, that doesn't look like it came from the frozen food section. And it smells good."

Jack must have been doing rigorous exercise prior to coming home to build up all that sweat, and yet all I could smell were hints of body soap, laundry detergent, and a hot-guy scent that was putting thoughts in my head. Naked, sweaty thoughts.

I bumped him with my hip. "Back up buddy—Hot Stuff is in the kitchen and making magic happen."

He chuckled and returned to the counter and the groceries he'd brought and started pulling items from a reusable shopping bag with Max's company logo on it. Jack was nothing if not frugal. "My friend Lizzie is coming over this week. I picked up beer, a few appetizers, and corn chips. Noticed you were out."

My hands froze as I prepared a flavored ketchup, and I looked over. "You bought me corn chips? Why?"

No one bought me my favorite food, not even Sophia. She was always too busy complaining they weren't a part of the food group pyramid.

He shrugged. "You like them."

Shit. First the domestic shutting down of the house in the dark so I could go to bed first, and now this?

I pressed my lips together and checked the homemade baked fries I'd prepared, distracting myself. He'd bought me something—without my asking. Without my even pointing out that I liked it. He just noticed that I did and got me more.

This was a slippery slope, and it was already too late because I'd fallen half in love with him.

"When will food be ready?" he asked, running a hand through damp, wavy locks.

"Soon," I said, my voice shaky. I was suddenly incredibly nervous. When had I started to fall in love with Jack?

"I'm taking a shower." He headed toward the hallway. His haggard T-shirt was thin from overuse and giving me an indecent view of his back muscles. So now I had the visual of his body through his tee and the knowledge he was getting naked in a minute. Not to mention the falling in love part. I'd never been in love; why'd it have to be with Jack?

He returned to the living room a few minutes later, showered, shaved, and with a newer T-shirt that didn't hug the muscles as much as the ratty one. I'd complained last night about his tee needing to be thrown out because it was too old. Now I saw the benefit of the thin ones.

I leaned over the dining table and set a pink peony inside a glass I'd filled with water.

He glanced at the place settings with blue cloth napkins I'd found buried in a kitchen drawer. I'd bet money Jack had never used those in his life. "Flowers?" he said. "To what do I owe this effort?"

"I owed you." I straightened a napkin nervously. "For last night."

He hunted in an upper kitchen cabinet. "You don't owe me anything." Then he glanced over with a wink. "I liked having you in my bed. You're a cuddler."

I covered my face, which had heated to a thousand degrees. "How embarrassing."

"Like I said, I enjoyed it." His lusty gaze shifted to one of annoyance. "Until you left without saying goodbye."

My mouth parted. "But I left a note. Didn't you get it?"

"I found it." He set what looked like a very expensive bottle of red wine on the table, then rummaged around in a drawer and pulled out a corkscrew. But not the cheap type.

This one was black matte with a polished wooden handle that worked like a crank.

He placed the corkscrew on top of the bottle, pushed down, then pulled up, and in one smooth move the cork was out.

The cheapo corkscrews I used would have left cork floaties, but the wine he poured into a glass was floatie free and looking delicious.

"Note or no note," he said, "I would have preferred to find you there."

I looked up to him staring, sending some sort of message my lady bits immediately interpreted even if my brain was slow.

My nervous system popped like uncorked champagne, and I set a bowl of sautéed brussels sprouts and bacon on the table, attempting to keep my hands steady. "But this is a platonic dating thing." I might be falling in love, but that didn't eliminate the potential combustibility of dating Jack long term. He was head and shoulders above anyone I'd been with, and he was Max's best friend. There'd be no escaping him if things went south.

He chuckled, the sound deep and rumbly. "It's not platonic." He made his way to the table and set the glass of wine down.

The wine, his words... Was he trying to seduce me?

I'd been seduced by his sweaty body and holey T-shirts. What would happen if this man actually tried?

It would be all over.

"Jackson, you said this relationship wasn't physical." I was scrambling at this point.

He lowered himself into one of the four chairs at the table. "It isn't. But if we decide to mix pleasure with business, even better."

"So this was always for sex?" I was pretty sure it wasn't, but desperate times and all that. Not like I hadn't just been fantasizing about his naked body.

He leaned forward, arms braced on the table, a tinge of atypical anger flaring behind his eyes. "You know it isn't only sex between us."

He was right. We'd agreed to date for practical reasons, but *I'd* agreed to see if all that initial attraction was fleeting. Only the spark hadn't fizzled. Not one bit.

I liked Jack a lot. And things were about to get hot. Because I was starting to think Jack might want me as much as I wanted him.

Chapter Twenty-Five

Jack

ELISE SET OUT PLATES WITH STEAK AND A VEGETABLE-bacon dish no self-respecting vegetarian would approve. "This looks amazing."

She scrutinized the spread. "It's a bit of a heart attack waiting to happen, but it should taste good."

Elise sat across from me, and I lifted my glass. "To roommates with benefits."

She scowled, but it was halfhearted. "Jackson," she said in warning.

I dug into the steak, cutting off a piece and taking a bite, pleasantly surprised at the flavor. "Why do you prepare frozen food if you know how to cook like this?"

"Because I don't like being told what to do."

"Trust me," I said, dead serious, "I've learned."

She peered over, considering, and I didn't like the calculating look in her eye. It made me nervous. "What happens if I sleepwalk into your bed again? I honestly didn't mean to last night, but apparently, I prefer your bed to mine."

My heart sped up. "Why don't you skip the sleep-walking and start out there?"

"Why? Because we're 'dating'?" She put air quotes around the last word.

"Exactly. Couples sleep together."

We both knew this arrangement wasn't normal, but I was curious how she'd respond.

Her pretty, rose-hued mouth twisted, and her gaze bored into mine. "You do have nice sheets."

"I can't take credit for that. Max refurbishes with nothing but the best."

She picked up a fry and dipped it in the spicy ketchup she'd been making when I walked in. "Did he pick out everything in this apartment?"

I glanced around. "Not the TV or any of the other electronics."

"But everything else?"

I shrugged.

"That explains the cloth napkins," she said to herself.

I held up the blue linen napkin that rested on my lap. "You found these here?"

She just shook her head as though exasperated with me.

"Huh, my best friend is more thorough than I thought." I shrugged and went back to eating.

She set her fork down and rested her chin on her hand. "You know, you and Max have a similar relationship to me and Sophia. Sophia is always trying to take care of me. Are you sure you can afford your own place? Why else would Max house you and pamper you the way he does?"

I tossed a fry in my mouth and chewed. "Because I'm charming?"

"No," she said without missing a beat. "That's not it."

I laughed. I *was* charming—my little black book said so.

But I found it funny Elise never caved to my appeal. "Then why do you think it is?"

"I think Max and Sophia need to take care of people. They're busybodies."

There was some truth to this. "Max knows I have no taste in décor. He likes nice things, so he stuffs my place with them so that they're here when he visits."

"You don't find that overbearing?"

I snorted. "Why would I? I hate shopping."

"Yet you went shopping with me..."

"Because you suck at wearing nice things. Your taste in clothes makes mine look good."

"I'm going to try to not take offense at that." Considering how she was shoveling in food while she spoke, I took it that she wasn't at all offended.

"Feel free to take offense. It's a fact."

"Rude." Her mouth was pursed, but her eyes were smiling.

I poured more wine into her empty glass. "Now that we're sleeping together—"

She pointed her fork at my head. "In the same bed! No one said anything about boning."

I held back a laugh. "Boning? Is that what you call it?"

"That's what Sophia called it."

"I have no interest in boning. You're merely a good pillow." I gestured to her chest. "Nice and soft."

She shook her head slowly. "I can't believe you, Jackson. When did you use my breasts as a pillow?"

"Let's see..." I looked up, pretending to consider it. "Every chance I got?"

"And what was I doing during all this?"

I gobbled down the last of my steak because it was delicious. "Stroking my hair while I was half awake."

173

She blinked a couple times as though she hadn't known she'd done that. "You have good hair," she said grudgingly.

"Feel free to run your fingers through it anytime you like. Or you can use it to direct me where you want me."

Her face pinkened. "I said no boning."

"Who said anything about sex? Get your head out of the gutter, Hot Stuff." She eyed me suspiciously. "But since you mentioned it, maybe we should kiss. You know, get it out of the way, in case you can't hold back and your lips land on mine tonight."

"Hah! As if that will happen. More like the other way around."

I took a swig of wine and refilled. The alcohol was loosening my tongue. "Pretty sure your lips were the first to cross the demilitarized zone way back when."

"I have no idea what that is, but if you mean to say I kissed you first that night—well, maybe. But trust me, these lips are on lockdown. I have them well under control."

"And yet you rolled into my bedroom last night like it was your own."

Her eyes turned to liquid fire. "Do you want your breast pillow back or not?"

I held up my hands. "Want. Definitely want." I studied her a moment. "Let's say, for argument's sake, our lips connect in the middle of the night. Would that be crossing the line?"

"Depends. Whose lips are in control?"

"Yours. Mine are at your disposal but won't cross the line without permission."

She snorted. "You think you can hold yourself back?"

I laughed. "Not if you don't. That's the signal everything's a go. But I think we should revisit the kiss. I barely remember locking lips the night you seduced me." A lie. I remembered every detail. "We wouldn't want anything awkward." Another lie. Being with Elise was the opposite of awkward. It felt weird to consider her not in my bed. Hence why I'd suggested we keep up the habit. "How about a kiss to get it out of your system? That way, if it happens, no one is surprised or horrified."

"Horrified! And what do you mean, you don't remember kissing me?"

I scratched my jaw. "It was dark. Maybe it wasn't that memorable... Better to jog my memory so I know what I'm in for."

She gulped down the last of her wine, and I grinned, not bothering to hide my pleasure at her feistiness. "You've just started a war, roommate. If I make your toes curl, what do I get?" she asked.

My breathing increased, and I squeezed my palm into a fist. "Toes curling. Mmm, you sure about that?"

She stood and crossed over to my side of the table, stepping between my knees. More than my fist began to stiffen.

I leaned back, admiring how fucking beautiful she was. Still wearing her Hot Stuff apron—she must have forgotten to take it off—hair thick and dark and draping over her shoulders in loose waves.

She leaned into me, and I gripped her hips. "What do I get?" she prodded.

My entire body lit up. I fucking loved a competitive woman. "Anything you want."

Her lips crashed down, taking my mouth like a marauding pirate, unchoreographed and slightly aggressive. She gently bit my bottom lip, which I adored.

I wasn't sure about the toes curling, but my cock was ready for action.

She leaned back, her face flushed, eyes glazed over. "Feel anything?"

"There's a stirring." Lies. I'd been craving Elise in my arms since the morning she slipped out of my bed like a thief in the night. She'd stolen something from me that night, and I wanted it back.

Sadly, the more time I spent with Elise, the more I realized it hadn't been my dignity I'd lost but something more. Like the heart I'd kept in a steel cage my entire adult life.

Adrenaline surged—the need to conquer thrummed through me.

I grabbed her ass with one hand and wrapped my arm around her back, pulling her in tight. She'd opened the door, and I'd be damned if I let it close again.

Chapter Twenty-Six

Elise

JACK GRABBED THE BACK OF MY HEAD AND TOOK control of the kiss, deepening it. His fingers in my hair, holding me, his lips soft but demanding... Memories of that night came flooding back.

Tremors took over my body as he brushed his thumb across my cheekbone, and the absolute sexiest hum came from his throat while his lips ran down my neck to my collarbone.

And I remembered the panic I'd experienced the next morning, worried that what we'd shared was too close, too personal. And terrified of what it meant.

But none of that mattered now. All I could think about was Jack and his warm body pressed to mine and how we could get closer.

His hand was on my ass, and then he picked me up and somehow tilted me back and eased us onto the soft carpet.

His hand slid to my breast.

I glanced down. "You said nothing about breasts."

"It landed there. Want me to remove it?"

"No. Might as well leave it." I grabbed his jaw and kissed him, loving the feel of his skilled lips. These kisses dragged me under, making me forget all the reasons we should keep some distance in this relationship.

Hand still on my breast, he gently squeezed my nipple, then slid his palm over the sensitive tip, making me squirm. He abruptly stopped and frowned at my outfit. "This apron is cockblocking."

I glanced down. "Huh. Forgot I still had it on. It's so cozy."

"Hot Stuff," he said, using my apron to address me, the way I'd caught him doing earlier, "you mind if I untie this in the back?"

I rolled to the side, giving him better access. A second later, I felt the tug of him unknotting the apron—and heard the telltale sounds of the keypad to enter our apartment.

What the...?

Jack's hand froze, and we both looked to the door. Then I scrambled out from under him.

He sat back, staring in confusion.

"Do something!" I whisper-yelled.

He climbed to his feet, but we both merely stood there, unable to break the mental fog of hormones.

Feminine giggles came from the other side. For a split second, I wondered if it was Thalia. Would Jack have given her access to his place? The thought set my blood raging.

Then came the rumbly sound of a male voice, along with a loud pounding on the door. "Jack, open up."

"Max?" Jack said.

He scanned me and straightened my blouse where it was sticking up out of the top of my apron.

178

I yanked off the apron and smoothed my hair before looking around. "Was it obvious what we were doing?"

His gaze snagged on my mouth. "You look good..."

My eyes flared. "Stop getting ideas and open the door."

Max and Sophia didn't know we were dating for real. All Sophia knew was that I'd accidentally slept in Jack's bed, which I'd done before, so that wasn't new. And that I'd made him dinner tonight. She wouldn't assume we were hooking up. Though we'd done that before too...

Jack gripped the back of his neck, then walked over and opened the door.

Sophia, Max, and a woman with reddish-blonde hair wearing a pretty short-sleeved black jacket and cream business slacks stood on the other side.

Sophia looked past Jack to me, and her eyes narrowed. "Where were you? We've been waiting forever."

A sweat broke out on my back. "Just finishing dinner." Was my voice quivering?

Soph stormed past Jack and set a bottle of wine on the counter. "Took you long enough to open up. Why'd you change the code?"

Jack grabbed a bag of what looked like groceries out of the arms of the other woman. "Elise, this is our friend Lizzie."

Lizzie held out her hand. "You must be Jack's new roommate and Sophia's sister. Nice to meet you. Elizabeth Crocker, but call me Lizzie. That's what the guys do."

This was the friend Jack said was coming over this week. But wasn't that supposed to happen later? "Nice to meet you too."

Lizzie looked around and turned to Jack. "This is a huge improvement since before your ex set the place ablaze."

A low growl came from Jack's throat. Usually, he

179

reserved his frustration for me. Probably had something to do with friends interrupting our...activities. "Must I be reminded of that every month?"

"Yes," Lizzie and Max said together.

Lizzie turned to Max, her skin fair with only a light sprinkling of redhead freckles. "This place has your touch. Did you decorate?"

"My designer decorated, but I gave her my Amex Black card. I also may have given her a few suggestions."

Meaning Max decorated half of it.

I looked between Lizzie, Jack, and Max. They talked like siblings. "How long have you guys known each other?"

Lizzie looked up as though calculating. "Since Max started stealing candy from the front pocket of my back-pack. So, what, fifteen, twenty years?"

"Something like that," Max said. "But you stocked that candy for me, so it wasn't really stealing."

Lizzie shook her head and turned to me. "You see what I've had to put up with?"

I laughed. "I can imagine."

"Back then," Lizzie said, "Max's ears were bigger than his head, and Jack was five feet, two inches. In tenth grade." She gave me a pointed look, and Jack dropped his head and groaned.

"Wait," I said. "Five foot two? Really?" I looked at the man in question. "He's over six feet now."

"Oh, yes," she said, "he is now. Poor kid grew seven inches the next year. None of his clothes fit, and he had a baby face and long, gangly limbs."

Soph snickered, leaning over the counter and smiling. "Lizzie is my new best friend. She has amazing stories about the guys."

"I thought I was your best friend." I frowned in mock

affront.

"We were born into our bestie statehood through blood. Lizzie is my not-blood-related bestie."

I could deal with that.

I turned to Jack. "So you were pretty small in tenth grade, huh?"

He crossed his arms. "I was a late bloomer. Took a few extra years to grow into this magnificence."

Both Lizzie and Max groaned this time.

"It wasn't all magnificence," Lizzie said.

Jack cleared his throat. "Much as I'm enjoying where this conversation is going, what happened to us getting together later in the week?"

Max took off his suit jacket and draped it over one of the barstools at the kitchen counter. "Lizzie dropped by on her way home from work, and we decided to bump up the party."

"And have it here?" Jack said. "Where it's tight and cramped? Not at your place?"

Max raised an eyebrow. "Do I detect a problem?"

Lizzie glanced at the dinner and wineglasses set out on the table. "Were we interrupting?" She looked between me and Jack.

"No!" I rushed to clear the dishes. "Not interrupting at all. I owed Jack, so I made him dinner."

I glanced at Jack on my way to the sink, and his eyes dipped down the front of my body, doing nothing to cool the jets he'd set roaring before we'd been interrupted.

What had we been thinking? That shit had escalated fast.

"Well, in that case," Lizzie said and grabbed the corkscrew Jack had left out, "let's get this party started. My first appointment isn't until ten in the morning."

Chapter Twenty-Seven

Elise

MAX AND LIZZIE HAD BROUGHT WINE AND DESSERT. The fine chocolate was Soph's contribution, of course, and for once, I wasn't the drunk one tonight.

"It's not my fault you guys were underedu...educa...ted," Lizzie said, slurring her words and struggling to get out the last one.

"What's she talking about?" I whispered to Jack.

"Woman stuff." He shook his head.

Lizzie pointed at Max and rolled into Soph, who was looking equally hammered, squinting and trying to open another bottle of red wine. "These guys had no sisters. Didn't know jack about women." Lizzie snorted. "Get it, didn't know jack? *Jack...*" She snort-laughed.

"Lizzie," Jack said and grabbed her wineglass. "You're cut off."

She pouted, then jammed a handful of cheese crackers in her mouth, grinning at the guys with her head on Sophia's shoulder.

Sophia was leaning into Lizzie too, so they looked like a pitched tent, holding each other up.

Max had his back to the couch, one knee propped up. "We learned a lot from Lizzie," he said thoughtfully. "All about feminine products and how to not say anything annoying when she was having her..." He waved his hand.

"Period?" I offered.

"That," Max said.

I chuckled silently. "Lizzie, you performed a debt of service to womankind by educating these two."

She nodded, still grinning. "It wasn't easy." Her mouth puckered as though she was straining for thought. "They taught me stuff too. Like how men are most dangerous when they're silent." She wagged her finger. "Beware of the silent ones."

The more food Lizzie shoved in her mouth, the clearer her speech, which was good, because I was getting a college degree on Jack. "What happens when they're silent?"

"They're plotting." Her face scrunched. "Or angry—it's a toss-up. Gotta shove 'em around a little." She pushed Max's knee as an example. "Get them to snap out of it."

"Does it work?" I asked.

"Don't encourage her," Jack said, but I wasn't sure if he was saying it to me about Lizzie or to Lizzie about me.

"For the most part." She sighed. "They need encouragement to talk. They have feelings. Buried deep in their testosterone-pickled man-brains, but they're in there."

I tilted my head. "Lizzie, why did you never date one of them?" Both Jack and Max were top tier in the San Francisco dating market, with looks and charm. Once I factored in wealth, women probably threw their panties at them from a block away.

Scratch that—women *did* throw themselves at Max and

Jack. Take Thalia, for instance. She was the reason Jack set up our fake-dating arrangement to begin with, which had migrated to real dating—but only for another week or so…

I glanced at the man in question. I didn't want to leave Jack, if I was being honest. But I couldn't hold on to him forever. He was a commitment-phobe and so was I. Plus, I had a life to establish, and I couldn't do that while mooching off a boyfriend. It defied my need to prove myself.

Lizzie's face comically contorted in horror. "You might as well ask me why I don't date my brother."

"Do you have a brother?"

"No," she said. "But that's because our rich parents are a one-and-done sort of lot."

Jack tossed corn chips in his mouth from the bowl he'd slid closer to himself when I wasn't looking.

"Is that true?" I said and moved the bowl of lovelies back in front of me.

"I wasn't in high society." He frowned at where I'd repositioned the bowl. "Only these two were. But I guess from their perspective, it's true. They grew up with butlers and nannies and drivers." He snapped his fingers. "What's the other one? The one I always teased you about?"

"The laundress?" Lizzie suggested.

"No, that one's extravagant, but practical. The other one."

"Christmas tree stylist," Max said.

Jack pointed at him. "That's it! I grew up decorating the Christmas tree like a normal American. Sometimes the lights were symmetrical, but most of the time they weren't. And the ornaments were always scattered willy-nilly. The first time Max came over for Christmas to help me decorate the tree, he was so confused." Jack started laughing, and Max was smiling too.

Lizzie reached for the glass of wine Jack had moved away from her, and Max shoved a bottled water in her hand instead. She shrugged and drank the water.

"Ugliest tree I'd ever seen," Max said. "You had to pick through the broken ornaments just to get to the halfway decent ones that looked twenty years old."

Jack belly-laughed. "Because they *were* twenty years old."

I smiled as the three of them laughed at old stories. I already adored Lizzie. You had to love a woman who put these two pampered bachelors in their place. Though Max wasn't much of a bachelor anymore, with my sister living with him.

"I can picture it perfectly," Soph said, smiling. "Have you ever seen Max load the dishwasher? He is so anal retentive about arranging the plates and bowls in corresponding rows." She wiggled closer to him and looked up adoringly. "Did you have someone do that for you when you were growing up?"

He dropped his arm around her shoulders. "What do you think?"

"You did!"

He seemed to be smiling despite himself. "We had a chef, and he had a crew of helpers. Of course there was a person who washed the dishes."

"Did they sort the dishwasher perfectly?" Soph asked.

"I wouldn't know," Max said. "I never washed dishes growing up."

Soph looked pityingly at her boyfriend. "Amazing. It's like you grew up in a foreign land, only you were two miles from where me and Elise lived."

"That's city life," Lizzie said, and fell backward in slow motion onto one of the couch cushions we'd thrown on the floor after they arrived. We'd decided to move the party to the living room, but our place was so small we'd ditched the couch in favor of the floor and pushed the coffee table aside. "Lord save me from my parents," she added. "They're going to give me a brain aneurysm if I don't find my own place soon."

"You're living with them?" Max asked.

"Unfortunately," Lizzie said, sleepily. "It was supposed to be temporary, but the law firm has had me on one out-of-town project after another. Also, my mom has an excellent chef who caters to my dairy issues."

"Why don't you rent my studio?" Max suggested.

Lizzie lifted her head. "Don't kid, Max. You know I love your building. Is the studio really available?"

"My tenant moved out weeks ago, and I haven't had a chance to get it painted. I should get my assistant on that," he said to himself. "In any case, I was planning on renting it soon."

"Sold!" Lizzie said. "It's mine. Don't rent it to anyone else."

"It's small. You sure?"

"Small works. Do you allow cats?"

Max chuckled. "It's your furniture Archibald will ruin, not mine."

"Arch is a gentleman cat. He would never ruin furniture. He only shreds my favorite slippers—a habit any decent Persian would approve of, because my slippers rock and are an irresistible plaything."

Lizzie rolled onto her side and faced me. Her hair was held back by a chip clip she'd stolen off Jack's cheese crackers. Keeping those crackers fresh was one thing Jack obsessed about, so I was waiting for him to steal the clip back. "Speaking of parents and moving out of their homes, what were yours like? Did you decorate the Christmas tree growing up like Jack?"

I supposed to the uber-rich, things like personally decorating Christmas trees was an anomaly.

"We didn't have a tree," Soph said, answering for me.

Lizzie half sat up and looked at my sister. "Jewish?"

"Nope. Just no room for a tree."

"In our defense," I said, "we had Christmas trees when we were younger, just not after our dad died."

Lizzie propped her head on her hand, her expression serious. "I'm sorry. It must have been hard losing your dad. And I heard your mom was recently sick? I spoke to Jack after she was hospitalized for the stroke, and it sounded terrifying. Is she doing better?"

I smiled, because this was a topic that I was happy to talk about. "She's fantastic. And she's very chummy with Max's mom these days. Can you picture it? We come from a low-income family, and Max's parents are, well, the opposite. It's wild."

Lizzie considered that a moment. "Kitty is warm once you get to know her. And she's gotten more so since they lost a huge chunk of money that pushed them back to normal rich people standards. What do you think, Max?"

Max nodded. "My parents were dumped by lifelong friends and supported by people they barely knew. It was eye-opening. Meanwhile, during all that, my mom reconnected with Sophia's mom, Brenda, whom she went to grade school with. The scandal was hard on my parents, and Brenda's situation put things in perspective. Health is king, and what they were going through was minor in comparison. Plus, my mom has hoarder tendencies like Brenda, just in a rich-lady way. I think they secretly talk about 'collecting.'"

Soph rested her head on Max's shoulder. "My mom's been really good about going to therapy and not reverting to old habits. I think having Max's mom in her life has helped because she has a good friend now. She'd been isolated for so long, and for whatever reason, Kitty broke through, and now they're scary close."

Max winced. "I hate it when they whisper to each other. Makes me nervous."

"Tell me about it." Soph shivered. "You never know what they're up to."

"I'm looking forward to seeing them together," Lizzie said cheerily.

"It's a sight," I said. "With my mom in her twenty-year-old muumuu and Kitty in her designer dresses. They absolutely love their 'dates.' I told Jack we should introduce his dad to them and bring all the parents together."

Jack's eyes grew round. "Don't you dare introduce them to my innocent dad. He's still getting over his illness."

"What illness?" Max said.

I looked to see Jack's response, because as far as I knew, he hadn't shared his dad's diagnosis with anyone.

Jack appeared cagey for a moment, before he cleared his throat and said, "He's recovering from cancer."

Chapter Twenty-Eight

Jack

MAX LEANED FORWARD, HIS EXPRESSION SHOCKED. "Cancer? You never said anything about your dad being sick."

I glanced at Elise. Having her here—reminding me that my dad was still alive and laughing at reality TV—made it easier to address what I'd locked away. "I should have said something. A part of me was in denial. It's one of the reasons I've been a hermit this last year."

Max dropped his head in his hand.

"But I thought you were a hermit because of your ex?" Lizzie said. "Why would you be afraid to tell us about your dad?"

"It's *cancer*," Max said, raising his head and looking at Lizzie.

"Oh—*ohhh*," Lizzie said. "Jack, you should have come to us. Why would you push us away?"

"Wasn't pushing you away," I said. "Just wasn't talking

about it. I was too busy freaking the fuck out over possibly losing him."

"I should have reached out to Tom." Max's expression was self-loathing.

"You didn't know," I said, realizing how messed up it was for me to have kept this to myself.

"It's been too long," Max said. "I haven't seen or spoken to your dad in months, and he's like a father to me. I should have known something was wrong."

Max had spent more time at my house growing up than his own. I felt ashamed that I hadn't told him. If I had, my dad could have had more emotional support. "There's no excuse for me not telling you, other than cancer being a trigger. I'm still worried about it, but—" I glanced at Elise, realized what I was doing, then looked down. "It's been easier to open up lately."

The mood had changed, grown somber, when this was the first time we'd been together in ages and it should have been a time to celebrate.

"I'll let you know the next time I'm headed over and see if you're available."

Max glared halfheartedly. "You better, asshole. I love your dad too."

"I'm going as well," Lizzie said. "You can't leave me out."

I smiled. "I'll message via a group chat and you two can argue about the details of executing the get-together."

"See that you do," Lizzie said, all proper, though the chip clip she'd stolen to contain her hair was listing to the side and sliding off, putting her professionalism in question.

"Don't leave without giving me back that clip," I ordered. "I hate stale crackers."

She rolled her eyes.

The party started to break up after that, with Max and Sophia saying their goodbyes and making their way to the door.

Sophia gave me a hug. "Let us know if we can do anything for your dad. Bring by food, clean his place —anything."

"I've got that covered, but he'd love to see you. Your sister has him wrapped around her finger, and he's eager to meet you as well."

"Elise has met him?"

I rubbed the back of my neck. "She helped me out one day after the person I'd hired to help with my dad couldn't make it."

Sophia smiled softly. "I'd love to meet him, and hopefully soon." She poked me in the side with a look that said she was serious. "Don't forget to keep us posted from now on."

Max tilted his chin up toward the living room. "You okay with Lizzie?"

Lizzie had curled into the fetal position as the party was breaking up and passed out on the floor. "I'll move her to the couch. I'd rather she stayed here. Don't want her going home this late."

"You know," Max said, "if everything works out, she'll become our neighbor. With Elise here now too, we'll have no reason to leave the building to socialize."

I nodded. "It'll be easier to get together. No more mass texting. Not sure there will ever be privacy, though, with us all in each other's business."

"Was there ever privacy?"

"Nope. Though Elise won't be here forever..." Her month was almost up, and I hated thinking about it.

Max's brow furrowed. "I thought she was your new roommate?"

"It's temporary, but maybe... I don't know." I glanced behind me, but Elise had gone into her bedroom. "She's stubborn, you know?"

Max chuckled. "Runs in the family." He slapped my back. "Good luck with that."

———

I CHANGED and got ready for bed. I hadn't seen Elise since Max and Sophia were getting ready to leave. She must be tired. I should give her space.

I didn't want to give her space. Was getting used to sleeping with her after only two nights of back-to-back crashing together. Decisions...

Maybe she wouldn't mind if I crawled into *her* bed? If Lizzie caught me, the jig would be up, but that woman was passed out hard on the couch and barely stirred when I covered her with a blanket.

I sat on the edge of my bed for a full ten minutes, considering what to do. One thing was sure: no fucking way were we sleeping in separate beds the last few nights we had together.

Decision made, I quietly exited my bedroom, careful to close the door to make it look like I was in there in case Lizzie woke, then crossed the hall to Elise's bedroom. I knocked lightly.

No sound.

I opened the door a crack. "Elise?"

Still nothing.

If she wanted me to leave, she could tell me and I would. As of right now, I'd assume she wanted me there.

I crawled into her bed, spooning her small frame. She had her hands tucked under her chin again, looking cute as ever. I buried my face in her thick hair, breathing in the scent of buttercream and strawberries.

She made a small sound, like a cross between a moan and a squeak. "Jack?"

"It's me."

"What are you doing?"

I tucked her closer. "About to doze off."

"In my bed? What about Lizzie?"

So she didn't care that I was here, only that Lizzie might find out? "I'll leave before dawn, promise. Lizzie passes out hard. She won't notice a thing."

"Mmm, okay." She wiggled her ass, scooting closer.

I encircled her waist with my arm, happier than I could ever remember being.

Chapter Twenty-Nine

Elise

I WAS CHATTING WITH MY FRIEND AND FELLOW epidemiologist Lakshmi about our plan for obtaining samples this week from a bunch of smelly football players at a local high school for a staph outbreak when Jack texted.

Jackson: Lunch? I'll pick you up.

Hanging out with Jack for lunch sounded a hell of a lot better than walking to the Starbucks around the corner. Who was I kidding? It had been a few hours since he'd left my bed, and I already missed him.

Jack had climbed into my bed last night, all stealth-like, after everyone left. The man smelled good, and I'd slept deeply with his arms wrapped around me. Too bad he'd left before I could get a good look at him without his shirt in the morning.

Elise: Sure. What time?

He gave me a thirty-minute window, which meant I needed to haul ass and finalize an email for the team on the staph situation before Jack arrived.

I was wearing a gorgeous lightweight beige sweater he'd bought me, along with dark gray slacks I'd coughed up and bought myself, so I was feeling pretty snazzy when he pulled up in front of the industrial public health building.

I rushed out and jumped in the car before he could get out and open the door for me.

He glanced over, a smile lingering on his lips. "Eager to see me?"

The truth would only go to his head. "Eager for food." But I was eager for his company, which was scary to admit.

He took in my expression. "Tell me we don't have a hangry situation on our hands."

I held up my thumb and forefinger to indicate a small amount, and he punched the gas, pulling into traffic expertly, if dangerously.

I braced my arms on the door and seat. "It's not dire, calm down!"

"Hell no. Have you any idea how scary you are when you're hungry?"

His expression was so serious, I laughed. "Can't be that bad. I'm way smaller than you. You could take me."

He looked over comically. "I'd let you win that fight because I'm a lover not a fighter, and then I'd lose a couple of limbs."

I grinned. "As long as you know who's in charge."

"That part's crystal clear," he said, a quiver in his voice to emphasize his mock fear.

For a moment there, Jack felt like my boyfriend. A really cute and funny one, whom I loved spending time with. It was exhilarating and also terrifying. I hadn't planned on this.

I cleared my throat and stared ahead. "So why the sudden lunch date?"

"Work lunch."

I glanced over and caught the stressed look on his face, then my stomach dropped. I'd hoped he wanted to see me the way I wanted to see him, but Thalia seemed to be the only reason Jack spent time with me outside the walls of his apartment. "Thalia's still giving you a hard time? What is wrong with that woman?"

He frowned and turned on his blinker before double-parking in front of a nice-looking restaurant. "I don't know, but I can't lose her. She brought in a major client this week that will hold the company up. Tens of millions stand to benefit from Environ, and I need it to get off the ground." He stepped out of the car, walked around to my side, and opened the door for me as a valet ran over and took his keys.

Jack pressed his hand to the small of my back and guided me to the entrance. Before opening the door, he said, "Sadly, Thalia's the best at what she does. I can't justify losing her."

I hated that he felt stuck. "She's certainly the best at sexually harassing you. Are you sure you can't hire someone else?"

He shrugged. "Took me half a year to find her. Besides, I can handle her."

"I can see that," I said dryly. "You're handling her by bringing along your fake girlfriend."

His expression grew serious. "*Real* girlfriend. You're mine for the rest of the week."

A shiver racked my body, and goosebumps flittered up my spine and down my arms. Jackson was hot when he got possessive. "Exactly," I said, acting like his comment hadn't affected me. "Which is why we're going all in today. We need to make sure that woman knows we're together."

"You sure about that? Because I won't hold back." He shot me a sexy look, which had me wondering what I was in for.

———

FROM THE MOMENT we entered the restaurant, Jack had his hands on me, and I was silently kicking myself for my overconfident talk about going all in. He wasn't handsy in a pervy way, but attentive. His fingers lingered lightly as we passed velvet chairs and thousands of bottles of wine along the wall on our way to the table. Then, later, he brushed a lock of hair over my shoulder when he leaned in to say something low in his deep, buttery voice. At one point, he touched my knee beneath the table while talking to his neighbor. To reassure me? To reassure himself? No one could see him do it, so I wasn't sure whom that had been for, but it had fired up parts of my body that needed to remain dormant for the remainder of the lunch. A lunch where I was trying desperately to make it clear Jack was taken. Because Thalia had seated her small butt directly across from us and was watching Jack like a cougar ready to pounce.

We had just finished eating, the dishes cleared, when Jack glanced at his phone. "I have to take this call. Will you be all right?"

The entire table of twelve or so people were chatting among themselves, including Thalia. All of them were sans significant others; I was the only girlfriend in tow. I gave him a supportive girlfriend smile. This was my job, after all, as he'd made clear by inviting me here today. "Of course."

He leaned in, and for a moment, I thought he might kiss me.

And then he did. Slow and soft. Not a peck, but something like it, only ultra-sexy in a way that had my heart hammering and my breaths coming out choppy.

Son. Of. A. Bitch. What the hell was that?

Before I could figure it out, Jack was striding away with the confidence of a superhot rich guy, and the entire room stared after him because that kind of power and assurance commanded attention.

I swallowed and stood on shaky legs. People at the table were engaged in one-on-one conversations or chatting in groups. They wouldn't miss me, and I could use a moment.

I made my way to the ladies' room, but as soon as the powder room door of the ritzy restaurant was about to close, Thalia pushed her way inside.

She took in my hands braced on the counter. "Everything all right?" Her expression said she couldn't care less if I was all right.

"Yep, all good here." I started to wash my hands.

She moved to the sink beside me and pulled out red lipstick. "My trip with Jack this weekend should be fruitful."

I blinked and looked at her in the mirror. Maybe it was the seductive peck Jack had landed on me, but I was suddenly feeling possessive. I hated the idea of Thalia traveling alone with Jack. And I really didn't like her tone. "You mean for a client? I wasn't aware there was a trip planned, but it sounds like things are going well with the company and investors." Kill her with kindness, that was my motto.

"Very well," she said and snapped her lipstick closed.

"Fruitful with investors and fruitful between me and Jack. We make a great pair."

Forget the kindness motto. I couldn't let her last comment slide. "Thalia, don't get any ideas. Jack is taken."

She smiled, mouth closed. It was the most sinister thing I'd ever seen. "You never know."

She turned for the door, and I grabbed her arm. "I'm only going to say this once," I said in an overly sweet tone. "Back off my man. I fight dirty."

Thalia seemed startled at the words if not the tone. She must not be used to people challenging her. She looked at my hand. "Do you mind?"

"I do mind. Sexual harassment goes both ways. Jack has made it clear he's taken, and now I've made it clear. He's not interested. Don't push it."

She delivered one last angry look, jerked her arm free, and left the bathroom.

I took in a deep breath and let it out slowly. The sexual fluster Jack had aroused was gone. Now all I felt was angry. I wasn't sure Thalia would take my warning, and it put me in a rage to see someone try to manipulate a person I cared about.

As I returned to the table, I saw that Jack was back.

He looked up as I took my seat, his expression happy. And then his smile faded. "Something happen?"

I met his eyes. "Just Thalia being Thalia." I smiled at one of the employees I'd chatted with earlier, who loved plants and talked about dropping by Sophia's shop. "I don't like it, Jack. I don't trust her. And now you're traveling with her this weekend?"

He glanced to the side as though confused, then back at my face, his expression softening. "I didn't even think about that. I should have told you. I'm not used to being accountable to anyone. I'm sorry."

"Not accountable. Just, you know, I would have liked to have heard it from you instead of her." Coming here as a buffer for Thalia and then hearing the things she said—it all had me tense.

"Hey," he said and nudged me playfully. "Don't tell me you're jealous?"

I pinched his arm.

He flinched, chuckling. "That one hurt. Remind me to block your hands when you're mad."

I scowled at him in irritation. "It was supposed to hurt."

Jack glanced at the others, who were deep in conversation. Except for Thalia. She was looking over every few seconds, watching us.

He slid the wooden chair I was sitting in closer to his side. "Don't worry about her. She won't take me away from you."

"You mean for the next few days?" My tone was cynical. "I'm sure I can hang on to you for that long."

He frowned. "Is Thalia really what's bothering you?"

I sighed. "Yes. No—I don't know."

Thalia's behavior angered me. But I was also tetchy about my and Jack's relationship and his reason for bringing me here today. I wanted to believe it was to spend time together, but now I wasn't so sure. Our relationship was ending in a few days. And for my own sanity, I needed to move into a place of my own to prove I could fend for myself. But I wasn't sure what that meant for me and Jack.

"If it's about moving out—" he started, and then, by silent agreement, everyone at the table stood, noisily scraping chairs over the wooden floor and cutting him off.

Jack said his goodbyes to the others, and then we made our way to the valet, his car already in front.

"About earlier—" he tried again after we got in the car.

I wasn't interested in talking about my feelings and why Jack only took me out when he needed to block Thalia. "Can we talk later? My head is pounding."

I reassured him three times that I was okay, and he finally let it go.

Minutes later Jack pulled up in front of my work building. "What are you doing tonight?" He looked determined.

"Going home?"

"Good," he said. "Don't get home late. Your boyfriend has plans for you."

And just like that, the butterflies returned.

Chapter Thirty

Jack

I'D BEEN LIVING WITH ELISE FOR ALMOST A MONTH, and in that time, my entire outlook had changed. I'd gone from a bachelor running from relationships to clinging to this woman for as long as she'd have me.

When Elise said she was confident she could hold on to me for another few days, it had lit a fire under my ass. I didn't want just a few more days. And I didn't want her to believe she wasn't important to me.

Elise was my girlfriend. Not a fake girlfriend or a girlfriend to have someone around, but the real deal. She was the first person I'd dated whom I saw a future with. When I considered it, a future *without* Elise didn't seem right. I couldn't let her go or let her think I'd allow Thalia or any other woman to come between us. And if any guy tried to take her from me—I'd fight for her.

I wasn't the least bit violent, but I saw red when loser deliverymen and rich society snobs lusted after her. I'd battle whatever and whomever I needed to keep her by my side.

Which meant I also had to convince my very stubborn, sassy girlfriend to stick with me. So I'd brought my A-game tonight.

I left work early and picked up the best wine in town on my way home. Not technically—technically, I'd sent my assistant across town during rush-hour traffic to grab it, but the sentiment was there. I'd personally called in a few favors from the best restaurants in town for part B of the plan.

Rummaging through the kitchen, I discovered that yes, those blue cloth napkins Elise had found were in fact mine, along with other tabletop shit I had no idea existed. What did Max do on his days off? Peruse home magazines? Who had time for matching salt and pepper shakers?

I set out the table settings, and the "deliveries" arrived. I'd texted Elise a half hour ago, so I knew she would be home any minute.

After quickly running through the shower, I returned to the kitchen to light stubby fat candles in expensive glass jars I'd found—*fucking Max*. I'd have to thank him later. The candles were romantic and helped set the mood.

The sound of someone punching in the door code chimed, and I took a deep breath.

The door swung open, but I was there first.

Elise looked up in surprise. "Uh, hello?" She smiled somewhat shyly. Thinking of that kiss from this afternoon? Wondering what came next? She was about to find out.

"The date starts now." I grabbed her purse, and then I grabbed her, picking her up with an arm behind her back, the other under her knees.

Elise squealed. "Jackson, what the hell!"

"Full-service date tonight."

I carried her to her bedroom, and she laughed as I set her and the purse on the mattress.

She looked up, bewildered. "Are you planning on carrying me around all night?"

I took off the heel-loafer things she was wearing—a pair of designer shoes I'd gifted her, which made me chuff with pride. "Nope, just getting you in your cozy mode to optimize the date." I gestured beside her to the folded boxers and long-sleeved T-shirt I'd pulled from my closet.

She ran her hand over the tee. "This one's super soft." She eyed me critically. "Were you hiding it from me?"

"You haven't seen all my goods yet, Elise." By the way her eyes widened, the message had been received. I pointed at a box next to the clothes. "Don't forget that. You have exactly five minutes until the dessert arrives. Hurry up and change."

"Dessert? I smelled food when you carried me through the apartment."

I looked at her in mock affront. "What do you take me for? I would never forget dessert. Three, to be exact."

She visibly jittered with excitement and ran into the bathroom. "I'll be right out!"

I headed into the kitchen, checked my phone, and noted the final delivery person was a block away. A light rustling sounded from Elise's room, along with a *thud*, and I grinned. She was shameless with food, mowing anything and anyone down to get to it. I respected that. And it made me happy to make her happy.

A few minutes later, Elise walked out wearing the boxers, the long-sleeved tee, and a new pair of slippers I'd bought her.

She posed, one foot out in front of the other. "You did not just buy me these." Her grin could light a city block.

The slippers were tan, with giant acorns on the top that flopped when she walked. Not the processed corn nuts she typically gobbled, but I'd passed one of those ridiculous sock stores, which also carried bespoke slippers, and decided they were close enough. "Do you like them?"

Her smile was so beautiful, my chest constricted. "I love them, Jackson. They're the cutest, and they're also soft and cozy." She proceeded to exhibit how comfortable they were by walking around the living room and looking down every few seconds, admiring the slippers.

If this was all it took to make Elise happy, I was golden. Because I had a million and one ideas that were Elise-specific. Thinking of how to please her was my new favorite hobby. "I'm glad you like them. But I thought you said you were hungry? Should I get rid of the food?" I was goading her, and it worked.

She glanced at the dining table piled with dishes I'd ordered from four different restaurants and quickly slid into one of the dining chairs. "Don't you dare get rid of the food!"

As if I would. She wasn't the only person in the house with an appetite. But threatening food disposal was a sure-fire way to get her to focus.

She was already placing the cloth napkin across her lap when I reached for the bottle of wine. "The food is for you. And if you will allow it, I'll have some too."

Her eyes swept the spread lustfully, and I couldn't help feeling jealous. "I'm verging on hangry, but I might let you have some. Are those empanadas?" She pointed across the table at a pile of crescent-looking pastries.

"Max claims they're the best in town." I hadn't tried one yet, but I trusted Max's taste.

"And sushi?" She looked up at me. "I've never seen you eat sushi."

"That's because my chef only feeds me frozen meals." My tone was one of dry accusation.

She grinned. "I've gotten better lately."

"This is true," I agreed. "The sushi comes from one of my favorite restaurants in the Marina on Lombard."

Elise held up two bamboo chopsticks. "You're even prepared! Did you buy these?"

I huffed out a snort. "Those are another of Max's contributions to the apartment. I should have asked him for an inventory before I moved back in after the fire."

Elise nodded. "When you get married, bring Max along for your registry trip. He'll make sure you're hooked up." Her face scrunched. "Actually, I'm going to bring him on mine too. I'll ditch the fiancé, and just take Max."

I felt a pinch of jealousy at the thought of Elise married to some other man. Unless the man was me—then that would be okay. I poured her a glass of the Rothschild Cabernet blend and one for myself. "You planning on getting married soon?"

Her expression was horrified. "Hell no. It's a hypothetical. Max is the perfect Jeeves."

"I'm sure he'll be flattered you value his housewares selection over his billionaire business acumen."

"Damn straight," she said with a twinkle in her eye. "I keep forgetting he's that wealthy. He doesn't make it obvious, given how much time he spends chasing my sister."

"It's nauseating," I said.

"Right?"

I reached for one of the empanadas and held it in front of her mouth. "Say *aaah*."

She greedily took a bite. "Hot, hot!" She fanned her mouth. "How is it so hot after being delivered?"

Right, that. "I paid extra on the delivery."

"Is this some rich-guy service us mere mortals know nothing about?"

I shrugged. "My assistant handles that stuff. I tell her what I need, and she hires the people to make it happen."

"I didn't know you had an assistant. Does she work for one of your companies?"

"Not exactly. She works for me, and if I need something done that can't be accomplished with the employees on hand at any of the companies, she takes care of it. I found Charlotte through Max, and Max has excellent connections."

She tossed another bite of the empanada in her mouth. "Rubbing shoulders with rich society people has its perks." She hummed, and her tongue darted out to capture a crumb from her lip. "So good." She caught my expression and said, "You may sit and eat too."

I was hungry, but not for food. Watching Elise was giving me ideas.

I sat and tried to focus on the dishes I'd ordered. I'd gone a little nuts, but I hadn't been sure what Elise would like.

She reached across the table and handed me an empanada, feeding me the way I'd fed her, and damn if she wasn't studying my mouth. *So* not helping the ideas swarming my head.

I chewed. "It's good."

"Just good? It's delicious. Max is a genius."

I frowned. "What about the genius who had it catered for you... *Shit.*" I pushed back from the table. "Hang on. I forgot about the dessert."

I rushed out the front door and found three boxes sitting on the porch—exactly where I'd asked them to be left. I carried them inside and set them on the counter.

Elise looked over hesitantly as she finished chewing a bite of spicy tuna roll. "I'm ashamed to say it, but I'm not sure I'll be able to finish everything. We might have to wait a couple of hours for dessert. But don't you worry," she said adamantly, "I'll attack those too."

"I would never doubt you," I said and sat back at the table, piling food onto my plate. "Whatever you don't eat, I will."

She smacked my hand as I reached for fritters from the Michelin-star Mediterranean restaurant. "Slow down," she said. "I've seen you feast, and I don't trust you not to eat it all."

I piled more food on my plate. "Get in there, then."

Elise murmured something about a human garbage disposal, which I assumed was a reference to me, then proceeded to shovel food into her mouth like a teen boy. It was a wonder where it all went.

And that was how Elise and I consumed enough food to feed a family of five.

Half an hour later, we sat on the couch, both of us leaning back because our stomachs were too distended to sit upright.

"I'm stuffed," Elise said.

"Too stuffed for dessert?" I lifted an eyebrow. I had zero interest in eating, for once, but I could muster up if she could.

She considered it a moment. "Give me thirty, maybe forty minutes. Then I'll be good."

I laughed. We didn't actually eat *all* the food—but we'd eaten way too much. That didn't stop Elise from saving room for dessert, which was one of the things about her I admired. I also doubted she'd wait thirty minutes before digging into the sweet stuff, but I was willing to humor her.

Approximately two minutes later, she said, "What dessert did you order?"

I ticked off my fingers. "Apple pie from a famed pie house, milkshakes from Moe's Diner that have been kept on dry ice—"

She sat forward. "Milkshakes?"

"There's more."

Elise laughed. "It's a good thing our relationship is almost over, or I'd be the size of a whale after another month of dating you."

I flinched, not liking the sound of that. Time to redouble my efforts. "You'd be a cute whale."

"Stop teasing me and get to the last dessert."

"Limoncello and raspberry cake. Full size. Not the minis we had at the dinner party that one night."

She smiled sweetly. "You remembered how much I liked those?"

"Maybe." I may have taken several notes on Elise's likes and dislikes.

She leaned forward on the couch and covered her head, then moaned. "My belly aches, but I can't pass up Moe's and limoncello raspberry." She dropped her hands and looked up. "You are a cruel, cruel man."

I stood and reached for her hand, pulling her up. "Just have a bite or two."

She followed me into the kitchen and leaned against the counter where the dessert boxes sat. "I'm willing to sacrifice my stomach if you are."

I didn't bother with finery and simply pulled out fresh forks, took a giant scoop of the cake, then held it out for her.

"Classy, Jackson," she mumbled as her mouth consumed that giant bite and her eyes rolled into the back of her head.

After the cake, we let our stomachs digest with a couple of episodes of trashy dating reality TV. About an hour later, I brought over the Moe's milkshake and sank beside her on the couch.

Her eyes widened and she ogled the inside of the carton. "It's chocolate mint?" She reached for the spoon in my hand and took a scoop—the shake was too thick to drink. "I love you, Jackson, have I said that yet?"

She was joking, but it was a start. "Only with your eyes."

She chuckled, then her gaze took in my face. I wasn't upset, but I wasn't laughing either. I was waiting. Consuming cold milkshake and waiting...

Elise leaned over and pecked me on the cheek. "Thank you. For everything. This was the best non-date I've ever had."

"Real date, Elise. Also, that kiss was a few inches to the left. You should try again."

She smiled with a gleam in her eye. "Was my aim off? Let me fix that." She leaned in and kissed me lightly on the lips.

I reached for her waist and held her close. "You've got some ice cream on your mouth. Let me get that for you."

I kissed her full bottom lip, sucking it just a touch and pulling her flush against my chest. "Next phase of the date begins now." I scooped her into my arms and carried her to my bedroom.

Chapter Thirty-One

Jack

"Jackson! You said sex wasn't a part of the dating agreement."

I looked down at her as I carried her into my bedroom. "Get your head out of the gutter, Hot Stuff. I'm taking you to your favorite place in the apartment."

She glanced inside my room and rolled her eyes. "I've heard that line before."

"Have you not crawled into my bed in the middle of the night not once, but twice?"

She sighed. "Yes, but—"

"And both times did you not enjoy said bed with relish?"

Her lips pursed. "The first time a little too much."

I set her on the edge of the mattress before grabbing the TV remote off the nightstand. "Don't worry, Elise, I won't touch you. Unless you want me to?" I lifted an eyebrow suggestively.

She threw a pillow at my head. "Find something good on TV."

"Sure." I reached back, pulled my shirt over my head, and tossed it aside. At her stunned look, I said, "What? I'm getting comfortable. I don't sleep in a shirt, and this is my bed." I grinned at her flustered expression.

"You're seducing me," she said accusingly.

I leaned back onto the pillow, crossing my legs at the ankle as I flipped through the channel menu. "My seduction techniques are more subtle than this. You'd never know it once I started."

"That sounds alarming. Are you a spy or a lover?"

I shifted so my chest was facing her and continued to scroll. "I believe in subtlety."

"Right, like ordering four dinners and three desserts? Real subtle, Jackson."

I glanced over. "Feel free to get comfortable. You don't need to wear that stuffy T-shirt. You can take it off. I promise I won't touch."

"Unlike some people"—she glared at my chest—"I don't sleep without a top. Stop trying to get me to do bad things."

"I'd never do that... Oh, here's a good one." I stopped on an R-rated romantic comedy and looked at her innocently. "It's perfect for us."

She growled and covered her head with a pillow. "This is extortion," came her muffled words.

"You're free to walk out anytime." I faced the TV and got more comfortable. What Elise didn't realize was that I'd wait forever for her.

Something hit me in the side of the head a second before I realized it was the pillow that had been covering her face and that Elise was on top of me, grabbing the sides of my head with her small but strong hands. "You win," she said and mauled my mouth with delicate, plundering lips.

I tossed the remote and flipped her onto her back. "Took you long enough."

"You planned this!" She grabbed my face and started kissing me—on my mouth, on my cheeks, then back to my mouth.

"Enough teasing, Hot Stuff." I pulled her hands above her head and kissed her like I'd wanted to from the start, slow and steady and with a ton of bottled-up sexual energy I'd been containing since we met.

After a moment of drugging kisses that had my head spinning, I leaned back. "This okay?" It was always good to check. We joked, but I really wasn't in a rush, though my dick might disagree.

"No," she said and tugged at the shorts I'd been wearing around the house and that said dick was straining against. "Take them off right now, Jackson."

I leaned back, admiring her. "I love a strong woman." I slung my legs over the side of the bed and shucked my shorts faster than it took for her to run her fingers through her mussed hair. "Done. What else?"

She glared at my boxers. "The rest of it too."

"Before you've even removed a stitch?"

"Yep."

I grinned and watched her as I removed my boxer briefs. I wasn't modest, but she certainly was if her blush was any indication. "You doing okay there, Hot Stuff?"

She leaned forward and stroked my cock, and lightning bolts went off in my head.

"Whoa." I wiggled out of her reach and moved so that my waist was between her thighs. "Let's hold off on that for a minute." I slid my hands under her shirt and rolled it up on the bottom, watching her as I did. "You have soft skin."

"No, I don't," she said, her words light and airy and distracted.

"You do." I kissed her stomach and then one rib at a time, running my fingers across her belly to her side, then back up again. "Very soft."

Her head tipped back, and she absently gripped my biceps as I inched her top higher to reveal small, firm breasts. She'd changed into a sports bra at some point, which I carefully moved out of the way.

"But these are the softest part." I kissed her nipple, running my tongue over her areola, then pushed her breast up and sucked gently, licking. "And you taste amazing."

"How does a person taste good?" she said breathily.

I looked up until she focused on me. "Everything about you is to my taste, Elise."

She studied me for a beat, and I wondered if she understood my meaning. "You already know I like the way you smell," she said. "There's a reason I wear your clothes to bed, and it isn't because I don't have any. I could borrow from Sophia if I needed to."

"Really?" I'd never considered why she still wore my clothes. Figured it was a convenience thing, or that she didn't want to spend the money. And I didn't mind because it was sexy as hell.

She nodded, her expression serious.

That acknowledgement sent my heart racing. I scooted up and kissed her. Then I ran my hands down her sides and lifted the shirt over her head, along with the sports bra.

For a second, she was tangled in the clothes and giggling at the bra caught on her arm, and then it was gone and there was nothing between us. I stilled and enjoyed the feel of her skin against mine. I could die a happy man right now.

And then Elise grabbed my dick.

I groaned. "What did I say about that?"

She was grinning. "I forgot."

I slid the boxers she was wearing down her legs—and the woman wasn't wearing anything underneath. I looked at her with a heated gaze. "You've been naked this entire time?"

She blinked. "Not naked; I was wearing your boxers."

"But you always wear underwear underneath."

"Do I?" Her look was mischievous.

My mouth gaped. "The one time I asked you if you wore anything underneath the boxers, you said you did."

She grinned. "White lie."

I let out a slow breath. *Calm down, Townsend, or you'll unman yourself in front of the woman you love.*

Fuck.

I loved Elise. And she'd freak out if I told her. I wasn't the only commitment-phobe in this duo.

She was kissing me lightly down my chest, which would quickly speed up the unmanning process if I didn't stop it soon.

I scooted down and eased her legs apart before kissing up her thigh. "My turn." Before she could reply, I was already tonguing her beauty. "Tastes good here too, Hot Stuff."

"Don't talk while you do that!" she snapped, gripping my head and holding me there.

I pressed my palm lightly to her chest because she was getting feisty, and fingered her nipple while I tongued her, hitting a sensitive spot. She started moaning and rocking into my mouth.

I did not move.

Not one centimeter.

I'd found a good spot, and I was no dummy. I would stay there forever and pass out from carpal tunnel tongue before I budged.

A minute or two later, Elise saved me from a hospital visit by grabbing my hair and crying out her release.

I moved up, kissing her as I went, while her breathing returned to normal.

The dazed look in her eyes cleared. "My turn."

Chapter Thirty-Two

Elise

THE NIGHT OF OUR ONE-NIGHT STAND HAD NEVER BEEN crystal clear, because for so long I'd been trying to forget the emotions it had brought out. Plus, it had been dark and more about feel than anything else. But some things were memorable—like the orgasm Jack had given me.

Tonight's orgasm was even more powerful. Did the man have a magic tongue? He hadn't used that tongue the last time, and I realized how much I'd missed out.

"My turn," I said and urged him onto his back before climbing on top until I was straddling his waist.

Jack reached for the drawer in the nightstand, cursed when it didn't open, then grabbed a condom and quickly put it on.

He gripped my ass, and I shifted until he nearly entered me. And then I adjusted slightly and he did, slowly at first, his head tipped back while his hands gripped my hips in a way that suggested he was holding back. But I didn't want him to hold back.

I leaned forward and rocked my hips, setting a pace that had sweat breaking out on his forehead. "Is this too much, Jackson?"

"Don't tease me, Hot Stuff. I've got a lot of pent-up sexual energy for you." He flipped us so that he was on top and drove into me.

I squeaked in surprise, and he stopped.

"You okay? Was I too rough?"

I smacked his ass. "Keep going."

He grinned and thrust forward, kissing me gently and touching my face. I'd wanted to be in control of his release, but he was back in charge and ramping me up for another orgasm.

He reached between us and touched me while he thrust, hitting two spots at once.

I flung my head back on a climax so powerful I felt like my spirit had left my body. By the time I could focus, Jack was holding me, his cheek pressed against my forehead in the throes of his own release.

A low groan escaped his chest as he peppered my forehead with kisses I didn't think he knew he was giving. The kisses grew less sporadic, more targeted, until his body stilled and his lips found my mouth.

But he was still inside me. And he was still hard. "I see you don't have a refractory period."

"Told you, I have a lot of suppressed desire where you're concerned. I've wanted you from the moment you walked in the door."

I stretched experimentally beneath him, making sure my limbs still functioned. "The day I moved in?"

"No. When you came over to visit your sister after she moved into my apartment."

Wait—what? I tried to sit up, but he was heavy. "That

was more than six months ago."

He brushed a lock of hair off my cheek. "Exactly. Half a year of built-up sexual desire. Let me know when you're ready for round two." His expression was calm but focused.

The man was serious.

I tried to sit up again, and this time, Jack rolled to the side, but he kept his arm possessively wrapped around my torso. "You haven't actually been celibate since we hooked up...have you?"

He didn't answer. Just stared.

My jaw dropped.

"There were other reasons for my celibacy besides thwarted desire for you," he said. "My choice in women was dubious, as Max and Lizzie like to remind me. I was reassessing my choices when I met you."

"So you decided to not have sex...indefinitely?" The last word came out in a high pitch. "You're insanely hot. How did you manage to not date?"

Technically, when I thought about it, I hadn't had sex during that time either. I'd fooled around with a couple of guys, but either I got cold feet when things became more serious or I found something wrong with them.

He cupped my ass. "Glad you think I'm hot." He was staring at my breasts. "About that round two—I'm ready when you are."

I put my hand on his chest, holding him back. "Jack Townsend, what are you saying?"

He sank onto the pillow and sighed, running a hand through his rumpled locks. "I liked you back then." He looked over. "I still do."

"Which is why we found ourselves giving in to mutual attraction. But—"

He must have understood the question I didn't voice,

because he said, "I like you a lot, Elise. I want something more permanent."

He can't mean... "But this relationship ends in a couple of days."

"Does it have to?"

My eyes widened. "Yes! Or the living part. I like you. More than is wise. You're smart and sweet and funny, and some have pointed out that I don't measure up. But I'm still figuring myself out. I've always lived with my mom or depended on my sister. It's important for me to prove I'm capable."

"To others or to yourself?"

"Likely to myself, but that doesn't change how I feel."

He sat up, propped on his elbow, and his mouth firmed as he looked off. "Fucking Thalia. She knows nothing about quality." He looked back at me. "You can't be measured because you're better than me any day of the week. You're caring and strong, and I don't deserve you, but I want you. As for your needing time to prove something to yourself— I'll wait." He touched my bare hip lightly, but there was desire in that touch. "I'm a patient man."

These were words any woman would die to hear. They were the words I *wanted* to hear—but I'd be putting off the one man I truly cared about because I didn't have my shit together yet. "You shouldn't have to wait."

He studied me for so long I wasn't sure he'd respond. *Having second thoughts?* "Let me worry about that," he finally said and leaned over and kissed me, then stealthily tucked me under his body.

"Jackson," I said in warning. "We can't leave things like this."

"Shh," he said. "Enough talking."

Chapter Thirty-Three

Jack

I woke to soft curves and Elise's buttercream and fruit scent. I'd have to find her shampoo and start soaping my body with it so I could smell her all day.

I stretched and rubbed sleep from my eyes, then glanced down at the warm woman beside me.

Not beside—entwined with me like a pretzel.

Elise's leg was flung over the top of my thighs, one arm was tucked under the arch of my back, the other was over my stomach, and her face was pressed to my pec.

We must have slept like this all night, because my stomach was hot from where her arm rested.

I stayed like that for a while, thinking about last night. Probably the best night of my life. I'd wanted to ask Elise to continue living with me, but it was clear she wasn't ready for that. I'd have to settle for her moving out and then dating like normal new couples.

Sounds filtered back from the front of the apartment, as

though someone were in the house. My body tensed. *The fuck?*

Female laughter trilled, and I sensed Elise wake beside me.

She lifted her head. One side of her cheek was bright red from being plastered to my chest. "Who's here?"

"Elise!" came a woman's voice I didn't recognize.

Elise sprang naked from the bed and almost fell over. "Holy shit!"

I sat up and reached for my boxers. "What's going on?"

She pulled on the boxers she'd worn last night and dove for the long-sleeved tee I'd tossed across the room in my exuberance to remove it. "My mother!"

I'd never met a woman's mother before, and this was one I wanted to impress. My throat went dry. "Did you just say *your mother* is here?"

"Jackson, get it together. She's walking down the hallway!"

"Shit." I couldn't find my shirt, so I lunged for a new one from the closet while Elise opened the bedroom door, hair sticking up every which way. But it was too late.

I stepped outside my bedroom behind Elise and was confronted by two ladies of middling years staring at us.

"Mom," Elise said. "What are you doing here?"

———

Elise and Max's mothers gave us a moment to brush our teeth, but the cat was out of the bag. Elise had combed her hair and put it in a ponytail, but other than that, we'd been caught red-handed and were wearing what we'd worn to bed.

I made coffee and dragged two dining chairs into the

living room, where the four of us sat on or around the couch.

Brenda, Elise's mother, looked between us. "Elise?"

Elise squeezed my fingers so tight they were turning purple. "Mom, you know Jack, Sophia's old roommate... He's my boyfriend now."

"Boyfriend? And he was my old roommate too," her mother said. "Hello again, Jack. Apologies for the uninvited visit." She turned to Elise. "Sophia gave me the updated key code and said it would be fine to swing by, but I think I'll knock next time."

Elise leaving via the fire escape after our first hookup and now a passionate night busted by mothers—we never did anything the normal way.

Brenda had lived with me and Sophia while her home was being repaired several months ago, but this was the first time I'd seen her since Elise and I started dating. And I was in my boxers after defiling her daughter all night. My God, this was the worst meeting of the parents in history. "Brenda, it's good to see you."

Elise smiled at Kitty nervously. "We've never officially met, Kitty, but I've heard a lot about you from my sister."

Kitty greeted Elise, then turned to me. "Jack." She grinned. "I see you're in good health." She scanned me up and down as though she knew exactly what Elise and I had been up to all night.

"It's been a while," I said. "I take it Karl is well?"

The awkward small talk continued for a few more minutes until Brenda finally stood. "Well, we better be off."

"We'll be late for yoga," Kitty clarified and tapped her Cartier watch. "Chop, chop," she said to Brenda.

Elise stood, frowning at her mother's outfit. "Mom, you can't go in your muumuu dress."

Brenda pulled up the hem of her flowy, floral dress and revealed women's leggings. "I came prepared."

Elise scratched her head. "I thought you didn't go to conventional stores." Apparently, Elise and Sophia's mom preferred secondhand, whether it be clothing in Brenda's case or fine art in Kitty's.

Brenda put her hand on her hip and lifted her chin. "I bought them."

"I'm impressed." Elise turned to Kitty and smiled. "Thank you for bringing her into this decade."

Kitty simpered. "Your mother has iconic taste, but some things must be updated, and sportswear is one of them."

Brenda looped her arm through Kitty's, and they happily made their way to the front door. But not before Elise's mother stopped and looked back. "I take it you'll be living with Jack for a while?" Her brow quirked suggestively, and I mentally cringed.

Ribbed over sex by the woman's mother. *My God, make it stop.*

"Actually…" Elise glanced nervously at me. "I'm moving out. I'll text you my new location."

I swiveled my head to Elise. This was news. She hadn't said anything about finding an apartment, and I'd wanted to talk to her about that.

The moms looked curious but didn't question it. And then they were gone.

Elise grabbed her head and groaned. "That was the worst!"

"Agreed."

Then her gaze zeroed in on the microwave clock, as though she were just now realizing something. "Shit! I'm late."

She was about to run off when I grabbed her hand. "Slow down, Hot Stuff. Where are you going?"

"I'm supposed to meet Sophia at the shop, and she's probably already on her way. I'll call you later." She reached up and kissed me hard on the lips, then rushed down the hall.

"Will you be back before dark?" I called and followed her back. "I have something I want to show you."

She stopped outside her door, her look coy. "That sounds mysterious."

"It's a surprise."

Chapter Thirty-Four

Elise

THE LAST TWENTY-FOUR HOURS HAD BEEN THE MOST amazing and confusing of my life. I was pretty sure I was in love with Jack, my mom had caught us post-coitus, and now I was moving out of his apartment. I'd signed a lease earlier this afternoon once I finished helping Sophia at the shop. After nearly four weeks of searching for an affordable studio, one had finally come up three days ago, and not a moment too soon.

I would keep my promise to Jack and move out after one month. That was the deal, and it was important to me to stick to it. I refused to be the girlfriend who used her rich boyfriend for perks like free rent. I'd worked hard to get my education and prove myself, and now was my opportunity to do just that. If we were able to survive our rocky start, Jack and I could survive a little distance. That was, if he hadn't changed his mind and was willing to date after I moved.

We'd done everything backward: the one-night stand, then moving in together before we were dating. I wanted to make a fresh start and do things the right way for once, but I wasn't sure how he felt, though his words last night were promising.

Jackson: Meet me at your old apartment at 4 p.m.

Elise: Why there?

Jackson: You'll find out.

So mysterious. Did he miss his namesake roach?

Now that I thought back, I'd been thinking about my sister's old roommate even back then, naming a cockroach after him. Which was funny, and proof of how much our night together had haunted me.

I grabbed my things and said goodbye to Soph before catching a bus that put me a couple of blocks from my old apartment. Only something was wrong.

I looked at my phone to make sure I'd walked up the correct block and had the right building.

A second later, Jack emerged from a modern stairwell.

"What's going on?" I asked, glancing at my phone and walking toward him. "This is the right place, but the building's not the same. My old landlord didn't give a crap about the building and never fixed anything. But this looks brand new."

He met me in front and faced the building. "It's been remodeled. Do you like it?"

The exterior had been given a light taupe paint job—no, more than that. It had been re-stuccoed with a smooth surface where once there'd been cracks. And the old wrought-iron stairwell had been replaced with modern black railing. Someone had also torn out the concrete in front and planted hearty Mediterranean trees I recognized from working with Sophia. There was construction still being done on one side, but otherwise, the building looked almost brand new. "I can't believe this is the same place. It's actually cute and modern now."

"No more roaches," Jack agreed. "You want to look inside?"

We climbed the swanky new stairs and passed a family on their way down. People were living here, but the apartment I'd rented was empty, according to Jack.

"How do you know it's empty?"

He punched in a code to a digital lock that hadn't been there before and opened the door. "I just do."

My breath caught. The place was beautiful, and that wasn't a word I would have associated with this apartment when I rented it. There was fresh paint, crown molding, new hardwood flooring throughout, and a small but bright new kitchen with stainless-steel appliances and elegant white cabinets. I rushed back out to check the number on the glossy black door. "Is this really my old apartment? There's no smell, and it's charming."

Jack nodded. "Same unit, different neighbor. Turns out the one you didn't like had a small hydroponic weed farm growing in his apartment, causing the moisture issues."

I looked up and sighed. "That explains a lot. But how do you know all this? Did you help them remodel?"

He waggled his head. "Not exactly. I own the building now, and I hired one of Max's construction crews, who were in between projects, to remodel."

"You own the building," I said dryly. "Like *own it*, own it?"

He nodded, seemingly nervous at my response.

I pinched the bridge of my nose. "Why would you buy this crap building?"

He looked around. "It had good bones and was in a solid location."

"But why *this* one?"

"Your having lived here was part of it. And I hate it when owners let properties get run-down. I've also been looking for something my dad can move into. I'd thought to buy a Victorian like Max's, but then I saw this place and figured it would do. I made an offer on the building as soon as you moved into my place." He looked out the window to the scaffolding. "We closed within a week and have been working on it ever since. Still waiting on the elevator installation and a couple other items."

"An elevator?" I threw my hands up. "Jackson, how can you afford a freaking building?"

"I've explained this. I've been lucky in business."

"This isn't luck. You bought an entire building on a whim. The cost of remodeling as fast as you did... That must have cost a fortune too."

———

I'D NEVER HAD to point out my net worth. Most people—usually the wrong ones—already knew, the sneaky bastards. After the first billion, I stopped paying much attention. Anything above that seemed ridiculous, so I left it to my accountant and Max to oversee things.

The point being, I understood Elise's reaction. I'd have the same one if I were in her shoes. But I didn't want any secrets with her. "I'm not the richest man alive, but as of the last time I checked, I have about eleven billion in assets."

She stopped talking and her jaw dropped. She stood like that for a solid thirty seconds, and I began to worry. "Elise?"

"I'm sorry, I thought you said you have eleven billion dollars." She laughed nervously. "You must have meant million—eleven million, right? Though that's still a lot."

Shit. "You heard correctly. Is that a problem?"

She blinked rapidly and started to pace, smacking her feet on the new hardwood. "Is that a *problem*?" Her voice had turned maniacal. "Are you kidding me, Jack? You live in a small apartment in your best friend's Victorian. How can you have that much money? You're not spending it."

"I spend it on new businesses." I glanced around. "And on real estate, as you can see. I like living in Max's Victorian. He has good taste, and I'm nothing if not practical."

She stopped her pacing, her expression pleading. "Jackson, please tell me you aren't a billionaire cash-hoarding asshole?"

Okay, this was a first. Usually, whomever I dated wanted me to take them to Lake Como on Max's private jet, because they knew enough about me and Max to know I could afford it. "It's obnoxious, which is why I don't talk about money. I try not to think about it. But don't forget, money can make positive change too. I have an entire foundation that gives an astronomical amount of cash to charities and supports thousands of scholarships each year. It's put to good use."

She grabbed her head, eyes wide. "I don't even know how someone becomes this rich. Are you some kind of genius?"

"Uh... No?"

"You're lying! I can see it in your eyes!"

I stepped forward and reached for her hands, pulling them down. "I've been able to give billions to programs that help people, and that's the best part about being rich."

"Please don't mention the *b*-word. Let's just call it the *m*-word."

"Millions?"

"Yes, that. It's a lot, but I can wrap my head around it."

"Don't you want to fly on my private jet to the Bahamas?" I teased. "My exes found that to be the biggest perk to dating me."

"I think we've established I'm not like your exes. And what do you mean, private jet? Do you have one?"

"No."

"Then why would you suggest it?"

"Max owns one, so we share. It might be fun to go on a trip somewhere exotic with Sophia and Max."

She breathed in and let it out slowly, as though to calm herself. "So you're going to let Max use his own jet, and you want to take a couples trip on it? Does this sound the least bit normal?"

I glanced up. "Suppose not. Wasn't normal for me either in the beginning, but it is now. As for letting Max use his jet, what can I say? I'm generous like that."

Her mouth twisted, but I detected a smile. "It's a good thing you're cute and wear sweatpants and aren't fussy. I have no use for fussy, rich boyfriends."

I pulled her to me. It was the first time I'd had her in my arms since she got here, and it made everything better, even telling her the dirty truth about my wealth. "I never under-stood how Max and his family accumulated so much money. Then I built my own fortune. Now I understand that rich people hold their money in assets instead of houses filled with cash. It comes and goes if you're not good at managing it. So far, I've been pretty good."

"Pretty good?" She waved her hand around. "What am I supposed to do with this?"

Her question was facetious, but I answered honestly. "I brought you here to ask if you'd consider moving in."

"To my old studio apartment?"

"If you wish. Or you could skip the studio and move a few floors upstairs into one of the three-bedrooms with me. It's more spacious. Eventually, I'll get my dad into the building too, where I can keep an eye on him."

She smiled softly, and her shoulders relaxed. "You're a good son, Jack."

"And a good boyfriend?"

She bit her lip, and the tension behind her eyes worried me. "A wonderful boyfriend. But I can't move in here. I need my own accomplishments." She laughed sardonically. "Sadly, mine consist of paying my own rent, but it's an important rite of passage. Does that make sense?"

I gave her a small smile. "It does, and I understand."

"Do you still want to date even if I move out to get my life together?"

I made a disgruntled sound. "I'm not happy about it, but if it's what you need, I can deal. And of course I want to date you. I said I'd wait as long as it takes."

She leaned up and kissed me on the mouth and then wiggled her nose. "I think I can still smell curry. Wouldn't the renovations have removed the smell?"

"Oh, that. I paid to move the tenants and their things out during construction. No one who cooks curry that good should live in the dump this place used to be. The family came back to a better apartment, but I kept the rent the same. Your old neighbor must be making dinner."

She reached up and cupped my cheek. "What am I going to do with you, Jackson? Who even does this?"

"A reluctant billionaire?"

She laughed and squeezed my waist, pressing her body to mine. "I guess I can live with that."

Chapter Thirty-Five

Jack

ELISE MOVING OUT SUCKED. I'D WANTED HER TO EITHER stay or move into the building I'd bought, but that wasn't what she wanted, and I realized my entire world came to a screeching halt if Elise wasn't happy. So Max and I, with Elise and Sophia's direction, helped her move into the shoe-box-sized apartment she'd found, and I dealt with the change. I also visited often.

I jogged down the steps to her basement apartment in the Haight District a month after she'd moved and knocked on the pale blue door.

Elise answered wearing my boxers, tee, and a sweatshirt from my closet she'd declared was hers before she moved out, because it smelled like me. "Hi!" She jumped into my arms and kissed me all over my face, and I carried her back inside.

The queen bed from the second bedroom of my apartment now sat beneath the main window of Elise's new place. I'd insisted that window needed bars because the apartment was on the lower level, and the owner was happy to allow me to pay for the extra security. Elise lived in a decent neighborhood, but you could never be too safe, and I wasn't taking chances with my girlfriend.

The rest of the furniture in her apartment consisted of a small used loveseat her mom had helped her find and a two-person dining table she'd bought from IKEA. No TV—not enough space. We watched TV at my place, or Elise used her phone if she was in the mood. We also routinely visited my dad and his mancave for episodes of whatever reality television he was into that week.

Sophia's contribution to Elise's apartment was a small hanging plant Elise babied like a child. But it was a happy child, with bright green leaves that made the place cheery. The shoebox was growing on me, and I found myself coming over as often as I could. Or maybe I just liked being wherever Elise was.

"Where's my dinner, woman?" I was teasing, and she knew it, or I'd have lost a testicle with that statement.

She slid down my chest until her feet hit the ground. "Coming, boyfriend."

Elise grabbed oven mitts off a kitchen counter that barely fit a microwave and pulled a glass dish from an oven that looked about half the size of a standard. This was what you called "efficiency living," but she had everything she needed, despite my bitching.

I peeked over her shoulder and breathed in deeply at what looked like a breaded chicken dish. "Going fancy on me? Nothing frozen tonight?"

Elise didn't make frozen food anymore, because if either of us wasn't up to cooking, we ordered takeout. I also suspected she enjoyed cooking fresh meals now that she knew how. And I enjoyed being fed, so it was a win-win.

She eyed me haughtily. "I made you something special so you wouldn't forget the woman who feeds you and warms your bed when you're off on your trip with Thalia tomorrow."

She placed the dish on the stovetop, and I wrapped my arms around her from behind. "I think about you all day, every day. Would be hard for me to forget you."

She twisted her head and smiled. "I must be special."

I turned her around and tucked a lock of hair that had fallen out of her bun behind her ear. "Pretty special. There's a chance I'd do anything to make you happy."

She beamed up at me. "You would?"

I dropped my forehead to hers, taking in a deep breath and letting it out slowly. It had been a long day at work, with Environ ramping up, and I'd missed her. When I lifted my head, she was looking at me with concern.

I smiled, basking in her expression that showed how much she cared. There was no one more warmhearted than this woman. "I love you, Elise. Even if you choose to live in a cube."

She pressed her lips together, and her eyes widened and turned glassy before she blinked. "I love you too." She reached up and hugged me, wrapping her arms tightly around my neck. She leaned back, smiling. "Even if you're a money-hoarding billionaire."

Sassy as ever.

I'd tell her I loved her a thousand times a day if that was all it took to make her smile. I wasn't sure why I'd waited so long to express my feelings. I'd had them for months.

I picked her up and set her cute rear on the counter before sliding between her legs and kissing her. "I love you," I said between kisses.

She grabbed my head, kissing my mouth and cheeks and eyelids, then back to my mouth. "I love you too."

The food grew cold.

Elise grew naked.

And we ended up in her bed.

Some forty-five minutes later, I padded back into the kitchen wearing nothing but my birthday suit to retrieve forks and the casserole dish for sustenance.

Elise sat up, and her face twisted as she reached for a fork and speared a chicken breast, taking a bite and staring off thoughtfully. "You better not have been trying to distract me with your love declaration, because I was serious about tomorrow. Don't let Thalia take advantage of you."

I sent her a disbelieving look. "Like that would happen. As for the declaration, it was past due. Being in love is new for me, so there are a few kinks to work out."

Her eyes twinkled for a moment, then she frowned again. "Thalia is going to try to take advantage. It's a gut feeling, and I'm worried about my cinnamon roll boyfriend."

"Cinnamon roll?"

She waved her fork absently. "You're sweet and kind, and that woman's a backstabbing, lecherous troll."

"Tell me how you really feel," I joked, but Elise was right. Thalia would probably try again, and not because she liked me personally but for the money and influence. Not that she'd get anywhere. I might have been a willing pushover in the past because I hadn't cared back then. Now I had no time for that shit.

I'd managed to put off the Napa trip a few weeks and skipped work get-togethers, but I couldn't avoid Thalia forever.

I leaned over and kissed Elise's cheek. "Thalia can't take

what's already been given away, and my girlfriend has me in the palm of her hand."

Elise stopped chewing. Then she dropped her forked chicken into the dish and climbed on top of my lap. "Who would have thought Max's commitment-phobe friend would give up his singlehood?"

I tossed my food in the casserole dish too and grabbed her sexy hips. "I seem to recall your skittishness with relationships."

"It takes one to know one," she said, then reached back and grabbed my dick. She shook her head slowly. "Still no refractory period, I see."

"There was one, but once the sheet fell below your breasts, my libido roared back to life."

She leaned over and kissed me, giving me the best view of her breasts in the house.

––––––––

I MET Thalia on the helipad the next morning, and she remained professional, going over preparations for the meeting and dinner party later that night. She'd memorized every family member and pertinent event for the attendees, as she'd been going to meetings in my absence and getting to know everyone. But I learned at the dinner party why giving her that much freedom had been shortsighted on my part.

Thalia looped her arm through mine as soon as I entered the dinner party, which was set in an underground wine cellar, with wine barrels lining the walls and blankets for the laps of the attendees because the place was kept at a cool sixty-four degrees Fahrenheit.

I tried to remove Thalia's arm, but she tightened her

grip and smiled at the owner of the vineyard, a billionaire who ran dozens of companies worldwide—the vineyard being a hobby and a convenient meeting place.

"Gregory," Thalia said, getting the man's attention, "my better half just arrived."

The fuck?

She grinned up at me. "Jack has a bit of mad scientist in him and can be a little scattered. I told you," she said to me, "the party was at six o'clock."

I peeled her off my arm and reached across the space to shake the man's hand. "I was told seven. My apologies." I glared at Thalia, who was ignoring my look.

"Not at all," Gregory Walton said. "I understand how these things go. My wife does the same thing to me. Tells me one time and forgets when it's been changed."

"That's not—" I started, but Thalia cut me off.

"Our partners can be such a pain, can they not?" she said, laughing.

And I did not think she was referring to me as a business partner. Mostly because she wasn't my business partner; she worked for me.

Before I could correct her, everyone in the room started sitting around a large mahogany table with crystal glassware.

I was irritated, but I'd deal with Thalia after the party.

I sat at the end of the table, next to Gregory, and we immediately began talking about the future of Environ. "This technology is on the cutting edge of climate readiness and would allow businesses like yours to grow with preparedness, saving hundreds of millions of dollars in loss prevention."

He moved his hand off the table so the server could set

down a salad. "It's fascinating technology. Not sure how we've managed without it."

I chuckled. "With expensive insurance premiums that continue to go up. Our technology won't eliminate the need for insurance, but it can be used to plan better, preventing climate hazards from affecting businesses and communities the way they have been."

"That's what we like to hear," he said and grinned at his wife beside him. She was attractive, wearing a sparkly black dress and gazing at him warmly. "My wife here wants more accountability. Wants us to leave more of a positive mark."

I grinned and nodded. "That's what I want too, and my girlfriend would agree as well."

Gregory glanced at Thalia a few seats down. "She's a go-getter, that one."

"Oh no," I said. "Thalia isn't my girlfriend."

Gregory turned to his wife, and they both looked over in confusion. "My apologies. We assumed by the way she spoke of you over the last few weeks, and then again tonight, that you were a couple."

My chest tightened, and my head grew so hot I thought it might explode. First Thalia insulted Elise, and now she'd been plotting and convincing my business associates we were a couple?

It was the last straw.

"Thalia gave me her resignation today," I told Gregory and his wife, whose eyebrows rose. "She'll no longer be with the company. I hope that doesn't change our informal agreements this afternoon?"

Thalia had been chatting with the CFO of one of Gregory's companies down the table, but at my words, her head swiveled. "Excuse me?"

I took another sip of the rich Cabernet that had been

served. "I've informed Mr. Walton you'll be leaving us soon." I glanced at Gregory's wife and smiled. "Tomorrow, to be exact."

Thalia's mouth gaped, and she looked nervously around the table. Our conversation had drawn attention. Possibly because I was fucking furious and not hiding it.

Thalia stood, threw down her white cloth napkin, and left the room.

A gust of air escaped my chest, and I breathed freely for the first time in months. I hadn't realized until this moment how stressful having Thalia around had been.

I turned back to Gregory and his wife. "Now that that unpleasant business is over, shall we talk about moving forward?"

Chapter Thirty-Six

Jack

Elise had been putting in long hours since my trip to Napa, and we'd hardly seen each other over the last few weeks due to some epidemiological foot fungus outbreak—not really, but it sounded more interesting when I called it that. Now she was talking about adding hours at Sophia's shop.

Sophia couldn't seem to hire enough workers. That woman needed to stop being so successful so I could get my girlfriend back.

But all that chaos meant I hadn't shared with Elise the turn of events at work. I'd been busy hiring a new CEO, who started in two weeks, and I also wasn't sure how Elise would react when she found out what Thalia had been plotting.

Elise was protective, and I was looking out for Thalia's life, because my girlfriend might un-alive her.

I'd been patient since Elise moved out two months ago. Mostly. I only insinuated myself at her place every couple

242

of days. Which she didn't seem to mind, since I provided orgasms and occasional takeout—the first being her and my favorite. But today I was putting on my business cap and thinking ahead to our future. Plus, if she agreed to my proposal, I could see her all the time.

I knocked on her door, laptop in a work case draped over my shoulder, then let myself in with the key she'd given me because they rolled old school in her building.

Elise walked out of the bathroom with a toothbrush dangling from her mouth, her hair in a lopsided bun on top of her head. "I thought we were going out to dinner in your neighborhood?"

I cleared my throat and tried to act professional, but she was distracting me in one of my T-shirts without a bra. I persevered. "We have important business to discuss."

"We do?" She walked into the kitchen and spat out the toothpaste. "Like what?"

"Hang on." I reached outside the entrance, grabbed the projector I'd left there, and carried it inside.

She followed me into the living room/bed area and sat on the loveseat. "Jackson? What are you up to?"

"Patience, Hot Stuff."

I set up my laptop and connected it to the projector, directing an image on the biggest wall in the room, which was small. None of this was necessary, except one had to go big or go home, and I was going big.

Elise tucked her legs up on the couch and grinned at the wall as though we were about to watch a movie. "This is so exciting. You've never brought out your sexy projector. Is this how you convince investors?"

"Yes," I said, all seriousness, cueing up the first slide and turning on the bright red laser pointer I'd brought. "Only my clients are less stubborn and more practical than my girlfriend." I sent her a hard look with no heat behind it, and she merely laughed.

Clearly, I wasn't the one in control here. A man could dream.

"Please pay attention."

She folded her hands and sat up straighter.

"Reasons Why Elise and Jack Should Move in Together," I read and punched the enter button on my laptop to move to the next slide. "Number One: I love you." I looked over and raised my eyebrow.

"A good reason," she agreed.

I hit enter and pulled up another slide. There was no reason to have separate slides, but this was for dramatic effect. "Number Two: I know how to order food and feed you, and I provide other services."

She looked over, smiling secretively. "Other services?"

"You know what I'm talking about. Number Three: You like my bed and my skills in bed, which circles back to 'other services.'" I winked and hit the key for the next slide. "Number Four: I can't imagine a life without you, and I promise to support you and your dreams, whatever they may be."

Her eyes softened. "Jack, that's the sweetest thing you've ever said. Another solid reason in your favor."

"Thank you. And finally, Number Five: I fired Thalia a few weeks ago. She lied and told our investors we were together, and I wanted to toss her out the window. I decided homicide would be extreme, so I fired her instead."

Elise's eyes widened. *"What?"* She stood, flexing her hands like she was ready to strangle my former CEO.

"It was the final straw. I haven't heard from her since, but I've been told through the grapevine—my assistant— that she's already moved on to another wealthy boss."

"Eww." Elise's disgusted expression turned to one of sadness and she walked over and hugged me. "I'm sorry she did that to you, and I'm sorry you're out a CEO. What will you do? You guys were making such good progress."

Typical Elise—more worried about others than herself. "The company's doing just fine. Fortunately, the investor we were wooing had experienced a similar situation and totally understood."

"Good Lord, what is wrong with people?"

"I don't know, and I don't care." I pulled her close and kissed her. "I'm just sorry Thalia ever tried to come between us. I should have fired her the first time she was rude to you. No reason to keep a toxic person like that around, especially someone who hurts the woman I love."

Elise touched my jaw, smiling softly. Then she snatched the laser pointer and tossed it over her shoulder. "Moving in together is officially open for discussion."

"Really?"

"Yes."

I picked her up and carried her to the bed while she laughed. "Let's celebrate."

———

No official conversations had taken place regarding me and Elise moving in together, because we were too busy celebrating the opening of "discussions," and also because Lizzie's delayed housewarming party was a few nights later.

I picked up Elise, then drove back across town and parked obscenely far from the Victorian due to Saturday night crowds. I held my girlfriend's hand as we got in our daily ass workout walking up the steep hill to Max's building.

A couple of minutes later, I juggled a bottle of wine as our breaths left condensation puffs in the cool December air and Elise knocked on Lizzie's ground-floor door.

Voices streamed out from the tiny apartment as we waited to be let in, which meant Lizzie had invited everyone we knew, because her place sounded packed.

After a beat, the door swung open. "Helloooo!" Lizzie said and gave a deep bow, wavy red hair bobbing as she swung back upright. She was wearing jeans and a light green fitted sweater that made her pale blue eyes look gray. "Welcome to the cat-lady den," she said and waved us inside.

Elise and I gave Lizzie a quick hug, then walked into the crowded studio apartment. I couldn't see what she'd done with the place because bodies were strewn everywhere. Well-dressed bodies, but still, this place was crowded.

Max had finally gotten around to having someone paint and clean the studio, and Lizzie moved in a couple of months ago. She'd been traveling due to some asshole at work giving her the shitty out-of-town jobs, so the San Francisco homecoming had been pushed back until now.

I climbed over Archibald, Lizzie's black Persian cat, who was meaner than an angry raccoon, and wiggled past Max's parents and Elise's mom, also in attendance tonight, along with my dad.

We'd finally introduced my dad to the other parents, at Elise's urging, and as expected, they loved hanging out together. Not sure why they had to be here tonight, but whatever—it was Lizzie's party.

"Hi, Tom," Elise said and gave my dad a big hug.

He held her arms and leaned back. "Elise, my girl. You're looking lovely, as usual."

They chatted, and I slid past to greet friends Lizzie still

kept in touch with. There had to be twenty-five people crammed in an eight-hundred-square-foot space, but the alcohol was flowing, and Lizzie had outdone herself in the hors d'oeuvres department.

After an hour or so, I hunted down my girlfriend on a small couch in the corner. She was talking to a coworker of Lizzie's. Even so, Elise silently stood and made room for me on the couch, then sat on my lap, all while continuing her conversation.

After a lull, she turned to me and gave me a quick kiss. "How are your high school buddies?"

"Doing well, but Max was acting strange." I glanced at where he stood. He had a bead of sweat on his temple, which was entirely not like him. He was as cool as a cucumber in the most cutthroat board meetings. "You think he's sick? Should I say something?"

Elise looked over, but Max had walked across the room to where Sophia was chatting with the parents. He leaned down and whispered something in her ear.

Sophia appeared confused and continued to stare up at Max as he glanced out at the small room.

"Everyone, if you don't mind, I'd like your attention." He gazed down at Sophia lovingly.

I scooted to the edge of the couch, taking Elise with me, as though preparing for something, though I didn't know what. "What the...?"

"Is he—" Elise started before Max's next words cut her off.

"As you know, I've been in love with Sophia for some time. She is the most caring, hardworking, generous person I know, and she makes me incredibly happy."

Sophia's mouth parted and her eyes widened.

Elise slapped a hand over her mouth, nearly hitting me in the process.

Max dropped to one knee and said, "Sophia, I love you, and I want to share my life with you. Please do me the honor of becoming my wife."

Elise squealed, squeezing the hell out of my arm and bobbing up and down on my lap while the room erupted in shouts.

I glanced at Elise's mom, who was grinning expectantly, as though she'd been aware of Max's intention.

Max pulled out a black velvet jewelry box and opened it, revealing a fat rock Sophia didn't even look at before nodding her head and climbing onto his lap.

"Aww," Elise said, looking at me with tears in her eyes. "They are so sickly sweet, but I can't even eye roll. It's so beautiful." She hugged me, and I held her like that, wondering when the right time would be to ask Elise to marry me. Not now, but hopefully in the not-too-distant future.

She leaned back, and her eyes lit up. "Ooh, you know what this means, don't you? Society wedding!"

"I thought you didn't like high society?"

"Some of them are really nice. Plus, Max and Soph's wedding will have amazing food." She looked at her sister surrounded by people and worried her lip. "I want to congratulate her, but she's being swarmed."

Elise snuggled in close, brimming with happiness for her sister. "You know, Jackson, I've been thinking about how I felt the need to live on my own and why." She looked me in the eye. "I was thinking about it even before your proposal to move in together. And what I realized is that no one is independent—not you or me or Soph or Max. We all depend on each other for one reason or another, and that's okay. That's community, and it makes everyone happy to have others they can spend time with and reach out to when needed."

I squeezed her hand and smiled. She was right, and it was a lesson I'd been learning myself over the last year.

Her brow pinched. "I thought I was the worst person for allowing my sister to take care of me, but Soph depends on me too. I'm the yin to her yang. When she was getting ditched by boyfriends and friends who ridiculed her for where we lived, Mom and I lifted her up. We may not have supported her financially, but we were there cheering her on. I miss her, and I miss you. The one thing living on my own taught me is that life is no good if you're not with the people you love." She cradled my face. "I love you, Jack. I thought I couldn't prove my love without proving I didn't need you and that being with you was a choice. But I can choose to be with you and still need you, and that's okay... Let's move back in together."

I let out the air I'd been holding. "Finally."

"Finally?"

"Been waiting for you to say those words—not those precise words, but the gist. I was prepared to wait however long I needed to, but I'm happy you realized it sooner. I want my pretzel back." I touched the back of her neck and guided her head down, kissing her deeply.

She laughed. "Have you been holding out?"

"More like hovering and waiting for you to realize how wonderful I am."

"I realized that during our fateful one-night stand. Why do you think I freaked out and bolted?"

"Because I was too hot to handle?"

"Especially because of that. Pretty sure I can handle you now, though." She kissed my forehead, which was right at lip level. For some reason, the forehead kiss and not the lip kiss received a cat call from Lizzie, who'd apparently been watching despite the engagement commotion.

"Stop tarnishing the vibe of my cat-lady den!" she shouted. This was definitely drunk Lizzie behavior.

Kitty Burrows shook her head in the direction of Lizzie, whom she called "spirited," and my dad and Karl Burrows laughed while the rest of the party continued to crowd around Sophia and Max. Though I caught Sophia looking over eagerly at her sister.

"Sophia is looking for you," I said, and Elise glanced up. She waved and blew Sophia kisses, standing as though preparing to go over. "As for living together," I said, rising beside her, "we can live in my two-bedroom until we decide on where you want to end up."

"That's perfect." She grinned and hugged my neck tightly. "Let's congratulate Soph and Max, and then we can talk about our moving-in plans."

We'd started to make our way to Max and Sophia when a loud horn blared.

And honked in a succession of quick beats, followed by another obnoxious blare.

I looked out a partially blocked window—the one Lizzie was standing in front of with her arms crossed.

Her expression was pure rage as she stormed from the window to the front door.

The entire room had momentarily gone silent at the horn honking, and I glanced at Max, who had the same "oh shit" expression I did.

We'd done everything in our power growing up to never anger Lizzie, and we hadn't seen her with that look in years.

"This is bad," I murmured to Elise and held her hand as I followed behind Lizzie.

We clambered around partygoers, chasing after Lizzie.

She stormed onto the pavement out front, her reddish-gold hair like a flame behind her. "Hey, asshole!" she yelled to someone out of view.

I stopped near the door, keeping Elise tucked behind me, and Max and Sophia joined us.

"What's going on?" Max said.

"No idea."

I couldn't see the person Lizzie was talking to because they were around a corner, but her hands were on her hips, so it was go time.

"Stop being a parking whore!" she shouted. "You don't own the street."

"Damn," Max said, shaking his head. "The new guy next door got on Lizzie's bad side."

"He's screwed," I agreed.

The neighbor didn't know it yet, but he'd just started a war.

———

Curious about Lizzie and the mysterious neighbor? Sign up for my newsletter and be notified when *Neighbor Wars* releases! You'll also receive a fun bonus scene from *Roommate Wars* when you click the QR code below and sign up. Be sure to check your spam in case the confirmation email ends up there.

THANK you so much for reading *Roommate Wars*! Please spread the love by leaving a review or rating it, and by sharing the book on all things social and tagging me.

xoxo,

Jules

Also by Jules Barnard

About the Author

Jules Barnard is a *USA Today* bestselling author of romantic comedy and romantic fantasy. Her romantic comedies include the All's Fair, Never Date, and Cade Brothers series. She also writes romantic fantasy under J. Barnard in the Halven Rising series *Library Journal* calls "...an exciting new fantasy adventure." Whether she's writing about steamy men in Lake Tahoe or a Fae world embedded in a college campus, Jules spins addictive stories filled with heart and humor.

When she isn't in her sweatpants writing and rewarding herself with chocolate, Jules spends her time with her husband and two children in their small hometown in the Pacific Northwest. She credits herself with the ability to read while running on the treadmill or burning dinner.

Stay informed! Join Jules's newsletter for writing updates and receive a **bonus scene** for *Roommate Wars*:

Made in the USA
Monee, IL
06 December 2023

48406200R00152